WHO WE MIGHT BE

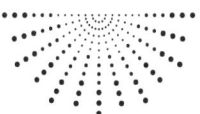

LINDA COTTON JEFFRIES

To Laura,
best wishes!
Ld C. J.

FIFTH
AVENUE
PRESS

Fifth Avenue Press is a locally focused and publicly owned publishing imprint of the Ann Arbor District Library. It is dedicated to supporting the local writing community by promoting the production of original fiction, non-fiction and poetry written for children, teens and adults.

Printed in the United States of America

First Printing, 2019

ISBN: 978-1-947989-42-9 (paperback), 978-1-947989-43-6 (ebook)

Fifth Avenue Press

343 S Fifth Ave

Ann Arbor, MI 48104

www.fifthavenue.press

Cover Design

Sally Day

Layout and Design

Ann Arbor District Library

for my mother, Elizabeth Cotton Jeffries, with love

CHAPTER ONE

*T*he crack of rifles broke through the rainy quiet of the morning. Members of the Old Guard on the hill across from the mourners fired a second and third time and then shouldered their rifles. Carolyn's face was wet with tears and rain, the drops mingling and falling on the black neckline of her dress. It wasn't a becoming one, but at eight and a half months pregnant, there hadn't been a lot of choices. She dabbed at her face with a sodden tissue before reaching into her purse for another. It just wasn't fair.

For two years she had waited and worried as her brother, Tim, served out his tour in a war zone, only to have him killed two weeks after he came home, hit by a drunk driver in front of his new US base. She looked at her mother sitting next to her, her face drawn and white with grief. Her father and her brother, Curt, were on the other side, both of them handsome and silent in their dress uniforms. They looked still and dry-eyed and she wondered when, or if, they would allow themselves to grieve.

She pulled out two fresh tissues, handed one to her mother and stuffed the wet one back into her purse. The pain in her back was becoming more insistent as she shifted in the folding chair, trying to find a more comfortable position. If her husband, Alex, was there, she knew he would have pressed his hand against the ache and eased the pain away. But, he'd been called out to a fire just as they were leaving for Arlington. She had pleaded with him to ignore the call, to help her through this painful day instead. But he insisted on going. She knew how important his work as a firefighter was, lives were at stake. However, she also knew the adrenaline rush that came with the job, the look he would get when the call came. Like a junkie with his hands on a fresh fix, no matter what plans they had made, they were never as important as the call to a fire.

The drive back from Arlington to her apartment in Baltimore wasn't long, but Carolyn felt the pain in her back increasing. She was eager to lie down. She called Alex's phone several times, but never got through. Finally, her hand pressing against the pain in her back, she unlocked the door to her building and stepped in toward their unit on the first floor. She reached out with the second key just as pain shot through her with a new level of intensity. She dropped the keys as she yelled and fell against the wall. The wave moved through her for what felt like an ice age before subsiding enough that she could reach down and retrieve her keys.

Once inside, she lowered herself onto the couch and took a deep breath as she tried one more time to call Alex. It went to voicemail, though, and the tears that she thought she had exhausted that day, began again. *It's too early*, she thought, as another wave of pain began. She tried to pant through it as she'd been taught, then thumbed in the numbers for a cab. She moved slowly, gathering up her go-bag, pillow and purse. She locked the apartment door and paused as another pain built and receded, then made her way to the stoop to wait for the ride. The rain from the morning had returned, a fine mist that left everything feeling damp. She leaned against the stairs, letting her back rest against the cool stone.

The cab driver was out of the car in seconds, carrying the bag and pillow in one arm, offering Carolyn his other. "It's going to be all right, Missus. The hospital's not far. I'll have you there in two shakes, you'll see!"

She managed to slide into the back of the cab but gave up on the seatbelt as he jumped behind the wheel. "Sinai Hospital? It's the closest."

Carolyn nodded vigorously as a new pain began. She gripped the armrest and panted until it ebbed away. The driver was a man of his word. Before she knew it, he was at her door, motioning for an ER attendant and a wheelchair. Carolyn couldn't be sure if she'd paid him, or thanked him. She hoped she had done both.

Two hours later, the contractions were coming one on top of the other and she still hadn't been able to reach Alex.

"It's time," her doctor announced after checking her again. "Is there anyone else we can call for you?"

It was the only weekend all year that her best friend, Janine, was traveling. She shook her head 'no' before grabbing onto the sides of the bed. "Okay, pant with me now, don't push yet." Carolyn heard the swish of the automatic door as they moved quickly to the delivery room.

Sometime after midnight, her beautiful little boy was born. Everything around her quieted down finally, and she was able to study his perfect face. His hand reached around her finger and held on until he drifted off to sleep moments later. "Your daddy missed something amazing tonight, little one. I hope it was worth it."

When she awoke a few hours later, the first rays of light were coming through the window and the baby was beginning to fuss. She lifted him out of the basinet carefully and opened her gown to offer him her breast. But he'd begun to wail by then and getting him to settle down and nurse was beginning to feel impossible. When the wails continued she reached for the buzzer to call a nurse just as one walked in.

"Good morning. I'm Asmita and who is this loud little guy?"

Carolyn sank back against the pillows.

"I don't know what to do, he won't stop crying." Tears were coursing down her cheeks as the nurse rested her hip on the side of the bed.

"Now, it's all right." She patted Carolyn on the shoulder before reaching for the baby and turning him against Carolyn's side. "We call this the football hold. Some babies find it a little easier to get started this way."

Carolyn adjusted her position, maneuvered the nipple back toward him and was shocked to feel his mouth settle on it. Quiet descended and she looked at the nurse in wonder.

The nurse beamed. "See, I knew you could do it. They always make it look like nothing at all in the movies, but it takes a little finesse to get most babies going at first." She rose from the bed and tucked a pillow behind Carolyn's back. "They'll be down in about an hour to do his hearing test so I think you'll just have time to eat once he finishes nursing. I'll check to see if the meals have been delivered yet." She walked to the door and eased past the young man who was standing there. He moved aside, then into the room.

"Babe," he came in and knelt down beside the bed, mesmerized as the tiny baby suckled, his right hand pushing against the thin blanket. "I don't know what to say."

Carolyn looked at her husband's eyes, damp now as he watched the baby. "Alex, where were you? I needed you!"

He rose and rested his hip on the bed. He wanted to touch her, to hold her close and marvel at the family they had become, but he knew he'd fucked up, big time. It had been a hell of a fire, a four-story building, already in bad condition, stuffed with tenants. His team managed to get everyone out and once the fire had been stopped they'd headed to the bar to celebrate. In the excitement, he'd dropped his phone on the floor of his friend's car and not seen or heard it again until he awoke, hung-over, in the back seat. He knew it was wrong to delay even further, but he hadn't wanted her to see or smell him looking like a bum. So he went home, showered and had a bite to eat before coming to the hospital. "Caro, it was a helluva fire. We managed to get everyone out, even the idiot that started the whole mess. He was trying to cook..."

"Alex, stop, just stop. I know the story. It's the same one I keep hearing. Big fire, have to be there. I get it, but you're not the only firefighter in Baltimore. You missed seeing your son being born. Do you get *that*?"

He stood abruptly, jostling the baby enough that he startled and began to cry. Carolyn held him against her chest, patting his back, watching as Alex paced the small room. "It was a fucking apartment building, a rat hole with over 85 people living in it, and all of them got out. My team and I got them all out. Do you get that?" Carolyn continued to watch him as he threw himself down onto the plastic lounger. "What do you want from me, Carolyn? I can't be in two places at the same time." He ran his hands through his hair, still damp it stuck up in dark, uneven tufts.

Carolyn deliberately lowered her voice, the way she would in her classroom. "I know what you do is important, Alex. But you have a son now, we're a family, and sometimes you're going to have to pick us."

CHAPTER TWO

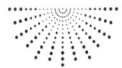

TWO YEARS LATER

*C*arolyn couldn't decide what to call what she was seeing. 'House' just didn't seem like a big enough word to describe what was in front of her. She wasn't even sure if 'mansion' fit. The place had looked like a fairly reasonable, upscale home until she'd driven along farther and discovered that what she'd seen so far was just one wing of a very large 'X'. She gulped. This couldn't possibly be right, she and her son could not have inherited something this massive.

Carolyn pulled up the wide, curved driveway, stopped and stared at the door in front of her. It wasn't even one door, it was four panels wide with etched glass windows on either side. She studied the simple key in her hand, baffled at the idea of it letting her into such a grand place. Taking a deep breath, she looked in her rear view mirror at PJ sitting high in his car seat. The drive from Baltimore to Pittsburgh hadn't been especially long, but with a two-year-old in tow, it had had its moments. None were as surprising though as what awaited them now behind the beautiful but intimidating door. "Ready to get out of the car, buddy?" A wide grin spread across his face and he began jumping in the seat.

As the key slid into the lock, the knob turned in her hand and she jumped back. A tall thin man in a beautifully stark black suit opened the door and ushered them in. "I'm Carolyn Jacobs," she uttered tentatively, extending her hand.

"Yes, ma'am. We've been expecting you. I'm Rupert Johns, the butler."

Carolyn felt put off at first, uncertain what to make of the stiff, proprietary air of the man, until she saw him smile and bend to meet PJ at eye level. "And who is this young gentleman?" He put his hand forward. Carolyn was surprised to see PJ shake it, rather than curl around her in shyness. A grin built on PJ's face as well.

Carolyn rested her hand on his shoulder. "This is Phillip, but we call him PJ for short."

"Peej," the little boy added on his own. The butler stood tall again and gestured them into the bright foyer just as an older woman entered the room. She was pulling off a flour-dusted apron as she moved forward eagerly.

"We're very happy to have the two of you here," Rupert intoned. "This is my wife, Helen Johns, Mr. Clark's chef."

Carolyn shook hands. "Mr. Johns, Mrs. Johns, it's nice to meet you both."

"Oh, now," Helen shook her head back and forth, her curly gray hair settling back onto her shoulders. "None of that. We're just Rupert and Helen around here. Mr. Clark never was one for formalities. We'd hate to start now." Helen bent down in front of the little boy. "Did I hear that your name is PJ? Do you by any chance like chocolate chip cookies?"

A wide grin stretched across PJ's face. He nodded as hard as could, looking from Helen to his mother. "Okay, Mama?"

"Of course, that sounds wonderful!"

"Great." Helen straightened. "Then let's get this tour started in the kitchen. It's always been the heart of this big place."

"Rusty," the butler called over Helen's shoulder to where a young man with bright red, curly hair was hiding in a doorway. He moved forward slowly and as Carolyn reached out to shake his hand, she recognized the familiar features of someone with Down's syndrome.

"I'm Rusty," he offered as he stood stiffly by Helen's side.

Helen beamed at the young man. "This is my grandson. Rusty, this is Carolyn and PJ. Can you say hi?"

He shook Carolyn's hand and then plopped down abruptly on the floor in front of PJ. "Do you like to play basketball?" he asked.

"Hoops," PJ called out and everyone laughed.

Rupert smiled and gestured to Rusty. "Come on and help me bring their things in first, then you can show PJ the basketball hoop."

Rusty got up eagerly and moved toward the door.

"See you in a bit," he called jauntily as he headed out the door. Carolyn felt her shoulders relax and some of her apprehensions drop away as she and PJ followed Helen into the mansion that was their new home.

It was so far from anything she'd ever known, Carolyn didn't know which was odder, the house, or the bizarre series of events that had led her there. That summer, at the end of the school year, she had been working at the Children's Center in Baltimore when a vaguely familiar looking stranger had walked into her classroom and introduced herself. Marybeth Rogers, her birth mother, had been forced to give Carolyn up as an infant when she went into the witness protection program to hide from the Warren crime family. Nearly 30 years later, with Walt and Jay Warren apparently dead in a plane crash, Marybeth had come looking for the daughter she'd never known.

For her part, Carolyn had always known that she was adopted, but that did nothing to mitigate the shock she experienced when Marybeth appeared. Later that week, she and PJ had gone to brunch to meet the owner of this home, her Great-Uncle Edward Clark. Suddenly Jay Warren had appeared, risen from the dead apparently, and Marybeth Rogers had been forced to shoot him in self-defense. Now, just one month later, he was being held in the city awaiting trial and here she was moving into Edward Clark's mansion. The week before they met, Edward Clark had changed his will, making Carolyn and PJ his sole heirs. In addition to endowing a large educational fund, he'd left his personal estate to them as well. After the events in Baltimore, he had returned home and died almost immediately of a heart attack.

Now she and PJ were here and she was still reeling from the whirlwind of it all.

Carolyn had been a military brat for so long that there wasn't any place that she thought of as home, until Alex, and their tiny apartment in Baltimore. Her adoptive mother, Angela, had returned here to Pittsburgh before her father's last deployment, but that didn't make her house a home either, especially given the state Angela was in these days. Carolyn worried about Angela, a lot, but meeting her birth mother that summer —even with all of the bizarre events —in some odd way had helped her come to terms with the woman she'd grown up with. Angela Jacobs had always wanted a little girl and there'd been a great deal of joy in the household when Carolyn and her brothers, Curt and Tim, were children. At least it seemed like joy at the time, but Carolyn knew enough now to recognize that her mother's depression and her dad's preoccupation with his military career had left sizable holes in that joy.

Carolyn caught her breath and couldn't help but stare. After the marble tiled entryway, a long hallway led on one side into a broad, beautiful living room decorated in varying shades of green from a pale, almost ashy color to the deep green of a forest. Two wide sofas sat across from leather armchairs while an enormous grand piano filled the room's far corner. Carolyn looked around her at the front part of the mansion and realized that her mother's house could have easily fit inside the living room alone. But all of those concerns could wait. She shook those thoughts off and passing by one beautiful room after another, she followed her son toward the smell of warm cookies and their latest adventure.

CHAPTER THREE

Shooting in Local Restaurant Leaves Two Wounded:
Baltimore Times, July 19, 2015
A quiet Sunday morning brunch was shattered today when shots were
fired inside the famous B & O Restaurant at the harbor. Taken into
custody was Jay Warren, reputed heir to the Warren crime family, recently
thought to have been killed in a fiery plane crash outside of Caracas,
Venezuela.

The article went on but Gregory minimized it on his screen and went looking for more recent news. It was the confusion in the restaurant that had allowed him the few minutes he needed to drag himself outside so that he could get to his car and onto the highway. He hadn't thought about where he was going or what he would do. He just knew that he had betrayed a dear friend and there could be no forgiveness for that. He had been surprised to discover that even after the series of beatings he'd taken, his wallet was still in his pocket. A quick cab ride had gotten him to his hotel and car where he'd checked out and then gotten on the highway. After that, Gregory had driven south as far as he could, until the lights of a 24-hour urgent care center caught his eye. He took the nearest exit and pulled into the parking lot just as a fresh wave of nausea hit. He threw open his door and vomited onto the parking lot. A mother and her daughter were just exiting the center when they saw him and rushed back inside to alert the staff. The next thing he knew, he was looking up into the face of a very young doctor.

"Well, there you are." She took the stethoscope out of her ears and looped it around her neck. "I was just about to call the ambulance and send you to the hospital." He struggled to sit up, her arm around his shoulders helping to balance him on the examining table.

"Thanks," he uttered weakly. "I think I might have a concussion."

"You think? I'd say a concussion, face and upper body covered with contusions, at least one missing tooth and a broken left arm." She ticked the items off on her fingers.

"Do you know what day it is?" She stepped back to lean against the sink counter and studied the bruised face. Gregory closed his eyes to try and think, swaying in the process.

"I don't know. I'm pretty sure I got here on Sunday. How long have I been here?" The doctor stepped forward to ease him back onto the table.

"You're right, it's Sunday afternoon. Can you tell me what happened?" Despite her age, the doctor knew a beating victim when she saw one. She was just curious how he would go about explaining it.

Gregory's foggy brain struggled with what to say and what to keep to himself. He figured he'd get as close to the truth as he could. "I got the shit beat out of me."

"And?"

"What and? I owed him money and I didn't have it." He

shrugged, which managed to send a fresh wave of pain through his battered head. "I appreciate the care, but I'm afraid I don't have the money to pay for it either." He slowly sat back up and reached for his bloodstained shirt. He held it up and thought better about putting it on. Then he looked over at the young woman. "What should we do, Doc?"

She took the shirt from him and tossed it into the trash, letting the lid thump back down with a noise that jarred Gregory and made him wince once more. "I'm going to bandage you up, set that arm and put you in a clean shirt. It's Sunday and our billing clerk can figure it out in the morning. Now lay down and be still." And he had. Once they released him, he'd gotten back on the road and driven as far as Richmond, Virginia. Then he'd done his best to disappear.

*I*n the month since then, he had risked using his bankcard only once and retrieved some money that he'd put aside for emergencies. He'd also recovered from the beating and gotten a job as night security at a small Mom-and-Pop manufacturing plant. They paid in cash and hadn't bothered to check references. He felt lucky to get it. He'd used the additional money to get a cheap laptop and some dental work to replace the tooth that had been knocked out. But now he'd grown antsy, worried he'd been in one place too long.

He told himself it was possible that no one was looking for him. After all, Jay Warren was in jail and he figured his henchmen wouldn't bother with a manhunt without Jay to push for it. The bigger worry was that the FBI might have a different take on the situation. Surely by now they were aware of the work he'd been doing for the Warren family and they had every reason to come after him for that. It made him sick to think that Marybeth now knew it, too. He was such an idiot. Why hadn't he been straight with her from the beginning? Of course, it was clear now. But then everything was clear now; it just wasn't pretty.

The day before, Greg had been in his room at a low-rent boarding house in one of the poorer neighborhoods on the south side of the city, when he spotted what could have been an FBI agent at the front door. No one spoke to the man, or let him into the building, and for that, Greg was grateful, but he knew that it was time to move on. Whether the guy was FBI, or part of the Warren family closing in, he couldn't be sure. He finished his Sunday night shift, collected his pay and drove south.

The junker that he was driving had been cheap. He'd stopped in Alexandria and made an even swap for his own car. No questions asked. This one ran fine, in spite of the rust, but he missed having air-conditioning. The North Carolina coast in late summer was intense. He had headed southeast out of Richmond, briefly considered stopping in Norfolk, but then thought better of it. Highway turned into two-lane roads that stopped and started through each small town. Beach traffic with its cars full of kids and towels, built up in waves that passed him going east and west, vacations starting and ending, he figured. Further south, he noticed that the countryside outside of Jacksonville had a poorer, sort of run-down look. He was able to find a fast-food joint just out of tourist range. The young girl working the drive-thru took her headphones off long enough to take his order and hand out the food. He took a long drink of the icy cola, reached for a fry and pulled into a space at the far end of the parking lot, unsure what to do next.

He had to admit he was already tired of hiding. It wasn't in his nature. Some people might have imagined themselves the center of some 007 adventure but not him. He missed his apartment and his friends, the macaroni and cheese at Lulu's, and a million other things about his city. Pittsburgh had been his home forever and nothing felt quite right this far away. When he really thought about the situation, though, the fact that his friend, Arnie, was dead was the worst part of it. He'd only had a small piece of Arnie's life, but he treasured it all the same.

But how to get back? There were so many unknowns that he struggled to find a starting point. It kept coming back to leverage. What kind of leverage could protect him from the Warren people *and* put him in the good graces of the FBI enough that they would choose not to prosecute him? He'd worked for Jay Warren, but would the fact that he'd been coerced into doing it matter in the end? Who was even left in that organization now that Walt was dead and Jay was behind bars? Wouldn't the FBI be focused on how to take down the rest of the organization and make sure that Jay remained where he was? The questions kept circling until he felt paralyzed, sitting in some shitty fast food parking lot with no idea what to do or where to go.

He thought back to his work for the Warren family and other than the bastard, Jay, the only individual that he'd had real dealings with, was his friend, Arnie, the accountant. Payoffs in the organization were still handled almost entirely with cash and other than the surveillance work, delivering cash was the main task he'd been assigned. Arnie Lowe, Greg could picture him still, sitting beside him at the counter in Lulu's, his laugh rolling out as they commiserated on the turns and pitfalls that their lives had taken. And then a look had passed between them and Greg knew that working for the Warren's wasn't the only secret Arnie carried. Was it love? He thought so, but even now Greg wasn't sure. Back at his apartment that night, they'd shared everything, come clean about their sexual interests, their gambling problems and the lock the Warren family had on their lives, the lies both of them were being forced to live.

17

"I'll tell you what," Arnie leaned back in the corner of the sofa, "I'm working on an escape."

"How, how could you get out?" Greg answered. "Twice I've tried. The first time I had my car stolen and the second time my apartment was blown up. I swear Jay knew exactly when I was getting close to having the cash to pay off my debt. Now, I've almost given up trying."

Arnie shook his head and set the beer bottle back on the table. "Money won't do it. It's going to take a different kind of power, information. I've been stuck working for that bastard for over 10 years. My wife doesn't even know it." He spread his hands wide as he talked. "I keep nothing at the house, nothing on me or in my car. All the records are protected. I don't want one of those fucking Morelli brothers showing up at my house, threatening my wife and kids. I keep it all separate and one day soon, it's going to be my ticket out." He picked his beer bottle up, drained it and let the conversation end. The time they had together was too valuable to waste talking about the Warrens.

Back in the parking lot, Greg took his bag of food and stepped out of the car, sweat dripping down the back of his T-shirt. He leaned against the front bumper alternating bites with sips from the cold drink. Hit and run, he figured it had either been Pete Turner or the idiot muscleman, Tony Morelli, behind the wheel. He was leaning more toward Turner though, knowing that was his style. Tony's brother, Vince, would have just blown up the car. Fucking loose ends, they were all just fucking loose ends in Jay Warren's master plan. Well, he smiled, Marybeth had found a way to stop him, but it certainly wasn't in time to save Arnie.

The smile faded and he shook his head in frustration, lowering it to study the rocks and litter around his feet. He'd stood at the back of the church during the service and slipped away before having to face Arnie's widow. Love or not, it left a hole, he could admit that much. Working with his friend, Marybeth, to find her daughter, getting to do real investigative work again, that helped to fill the hole for a bit, but now that was over. He looked around at the tall, straight pines that lined the highway across from where he stood and wondered if he should just walk in there and never come out. He was still carrying around the pain pills from his urgent care visit. They'd probably be enough. He could find some soft ground, lie down and look up at the trees and sky overhead, just be done with everything. Then, for the briefest second, he imagined Arnie's hand resting gently on his shoulder and he knew he couldn't do it. He had to keep going. It's what Arnie would have done.

Greg finished his lunch, walked across the rutted parking lot and stuffed the crumpled bag into a trash bin. Just as he tossed the empty cup in after, his eye caught on a brown road sign half covered by brush. He walked over and saw the words he'd nearly forgotten, *Hammocks Beach State Park*. Son of a bitch, he'd known where he was going after all. How was that possible? Had the concussion jarred something loose? He and Arnie had been sitting up in bed, half watching a football game one night, talking about their childhoods. Greg's had all been spent in Pittsburgh, the farthest he'd ventured had been Penn State for college. But Arnie's mother had been born in the south so each summer his family would spend a week along the North Carolina coast. When he'd gotten older, Arnie had asked to spend the summer there and he'd landed a job at the State Park to pay for it. He'd told Greg about the campground out on Bear Island and the little concession stand where he'd spent the summer helping boaters, and handing out snacks and bottles of Coke. Vacationing there had continued to be a tradition in his family, although he admitted that his wife and kids were growing less enthusiastic about the trip each year.

Suddenly, Greg remembered that he'd passed a big box store a few miles back so he turned out of the lot and headed back the way he'd come. Once there, it was easy to locate a small tent and lightweight sleeping bag, a lantern and a backpack that he filled with dried foods. He chewed on a piece of beef jerky as he settled back on the road to the state park. He had called ahead and discovered that there was a single campsite free and one last ferry heading out to the island for the day. When he got there, he emptied the items from the junker into a couple of overstuffed trash bags, and left it in the parking lot before stepping on board. Several passengers looked at him askance and he figured he must look like some sort of homeless person. Oh, well, he supposed he was, so he shrugged, put on a bit of a gruff face and was quickly left alone.

The ferry ride didn't take long. He enjoyed having the wind off the ocean in his face as he tilted his head to watch the gulls and terns as they moved around the boat, hopping from island to island. Once they docked, he took his time, watching to see what the more experienced visitors would do. He followed along as they walked in a ragged, single file line. There was a paved path about ten feet wide that was worn thin in places. It started out crossing through a shaded, wooded area before opening up into a flat expanse that crossed the width of the island. On the far side, nestled into the dunes close to the ocean surf was a bathhouse and observation area. There, an old wooden sign held a map of the island. He noted the number for his spot and then headed to his campsite.

The island was so much bigger than he'd been expecting. He walked along the wet sand between the waves and the dunes and watched as most of the tourists began opening up chairs and umbrellas. None of the other ferry riders appeared to be camping so he left them behind as he followed the shoreline to where site number eight was located. He climbed up a small gap in the grass-covered dunes and nearly tripped as the sand slid out from under his foot on the far side. He slid more carefully then, down the short slope to the campsite. There was a tall pole to one side, a bare, flattened area kept free of the dune grass for the tent and a small, battered picnic table that had needed repainting a decade ago. He supposed there was a good reason this was called primitive camping. The tent was a simple one that didn't take much time to set up. He hung his lantern from the pole provided and tucked the rest of his things into his tent. Then he set about exploring Arnie's old hangout and his new home.

CHAPTER FOUR

*P*ete was happy to see the backside of Jay Warren and his henchman, Vince Morelli, as they exited the tropical resort and climbed into the waiting taxi. He looked at the boarding passes in his hand, two for Doha, Qatar, leaving the next morning. The hell with that, he thought. Pete Turner had been working for Jay Warren long enough. With Walt Warren's death and now Jay a continent away, he was making his own plans. At the moment, he was eager to get checked out of their shitty room, so he texted Al as he walked. *I'm getting our things and checking out. Bring the car around front.*

It didn't take him long to throw the take-out containers in the trash and his few belongings into a worn duffle. As usual, Al's things were in tidy piles already in his suitcase. He tossed their toiletries into the separate bags, zipped them shut and then opened the door. Suddenly, an explosion outside the long hallway blew the exit door inward along with smoke and debris that smelled like metal and oil. Pete reeled back into the room, slammed the door and threw the bags on the bed. "Goddamn, shit."

A million epithets swam through his brain. Of course, their car had blown up, he knew it without even having to look. It was

Vince's style and he and Al were just two more loose ends. That must have been what Vince was doing last night, he thought, remembering how the big man had attempted to be quiet as he slipped into the room they were forced to share. When Pete thought about it now, he wondered why he hadn't been more suspicious. Well, fuck, how much cash did he have left? He took the money from Al's bag, knowing the man would not be back. Then he grabbed his wallet and emptied it of his own wad of bills. He took a second to scatter more clothes around the room and set a match to the bedspread before he pocketed his toothbrush and his phone. Then he thought better of it, broke the phone apart, and tossed that in too. He kept his actual driver's license but left behind the passport and license that he'd been using there. As sirens blared and hotel guests filled the stairs and elevators, he slipped through the frightened groups and out the opposite end of the hall. Some clothes, a haircut and a new passport were his priorities now. Then he'd figure out what to do next. It was past time for him to take charge.

CHAPTER FIVE

 r. Charles Wright was fighting off tears as he stood in front of the wide, opulent doorway. He rubbed his hand over his bald dome and told himself to pull it together. He and Eddie had been friends for more than 60 years. Edward Clark had been gone for more than a month, but this was the first time Charles had returned to his late friend's home. Of course, in Pittsburgh's exclusive Hartwood Manor neighborhood, a home wasn't simply a home and Eddie's was no exception. It sprawled across the ten-acre lot like a wide 'X' with each wing offering stunning views. For someone as down-to-earth as Eddie, it had always seemed like a contradiction, but as the owner of a dry cleaning empire that spread across more than 30 states, he could certainly afford it. Charles dreaded the stone-faced, silent movie butler who was always the first encounter in a visit to Eddie's. He straightened his shoulders finally, and rang the bell.

The door opened slowly and he saw the man standing tall beside it, but a fresh, sweet voice called out to him at the same time. "I'm so glad you made it, Dr. Wright!"

Carolyn came forward with PJ. "Rupert, we're going to be in the library, do you mind asking Helen to bring us some coffee?" she beamed at the man and Charles was surprised to see the smile spread across the butler's usually expressionless face. Carolyn directed PJ toward the butler.

The little boy jumped up and down before taking the tall man's hand. Charles couldn't help but laugh as he shook Carolyn's hand. "I didn't even know the man could smile! What other miracles have you pulled off here, my dear?" Carolyn laughed and put her arm through his, as they walked down the left wing toward the library.

"Oh, Dr. Wright..."

"Charlie, we agreed, remember?"

"Charlie," she smiled. "Rupert and Helen are one of the nicest couples I've ever met."

Charlie stopped in mid-stride. "They're a couple?"

Carolyn laughed again. "Oh, yes," She motioned him toward a pair of armchairs near the window. "They talk so fondly of Mr. Clark, too, between your stories and theirs. I feel as if I almost know him."

Charles looked around the beautiful room as he settled into the armchair. Three of the walls were lined with bookshelves, while a brass-edged ladder leaned on a rail that circled most of the room. The fourth wall was built of windows, with wide French doors that opened onto a lush garden. When Eddie was alive, they had rarely come in here, meeting more often than not, out in the kitchen, where Helen would fuss over them and bring them platters of freshly baked cookies.

"So, are you and PJ getting settled in all right?"

Carolyn shook her head in wonder, "I think there are a lot of rooms that I still haven't seen. After our tiny apartment in Baltimore, this is unreal. But PJ is happy. " She smiled. "Helen and Rupert look after him so well, it's wonderful"

"I think you've probably brought some unexpected excitement back into their lives. That's a gift, especially as we're missing Eddie."

She could see the sadness settle on his face. He took a deep breath and continued, "So, what did you want to talk with me about?"

Just then Helen entered, bringing with her a tray with a carafe, cups and a plate of cookies. "How are you, Dr. Wright? Anything else you need, Carolyn?"

"Good morning, Helen. I'm well, but, please, call me Charlie, after all these years."

Helen beamed as she poured the coffee and handed him a cup. "Charlie it is. Just give me a call if you need anything." She gestured toward the old fashioned phone that sat nearby, before closing the door behind her.

Carolyn laughed, "Can you believe it? I'm living in a house so big that it has its own phone network." She laughed again and sipped at her coffee. "Okay." She took a deep breath. "When you and I talked after Mr. Clark's funeral, I wasn't really taking in everything you said about the estate, much less about the educational fund. But now I'd like to hear more."

"Certainly, Eddie set aside quite a lot of money actually, to help special needs children like his nephew, Daniel."

"And has it already been determined how the funds will be spent?"

"Oh, no, not yet." He took a sip of his coffee and smiled at her, the sadness still so close to the surface that she could see it. "I agreed to run it for him when he made the plan originally, but he and I both hoped you and Marybeth might be interested in taking it over. Are you interested?"

Carolyn nodded. "I spoke with Marybeth and she's interested in a role with the grant side of the fund's operation. I'm interested too, but I have a different idea than Eddie might have anticipated, and I'd like your input."

He selected a sugar cookie from the pile and gestured toward her to continue.

"My background is teaching and that's what I'd like to keep

27

doing. My idea is to set up not just a foundation, but a children's center, here at the house, where children with special needs could be evaluated and their parents could receive help planning for their futures."

"You want to set up a classroom, here?" He looked around the wonderful room, imagining the tables scratched and the floor littered with papers.

"Well, not this room in particular, I see this as more of an office. I was thinking about the wing with the atrium, a beautiful room with lots of light that I think would make a wonderful classroom. And the rooms around it could house small conference spaces as well as a testing center and an observation room."

"Wow, you've really thought this out, haven't you?" He set his cup down on the tray.

"I have." She nodded. "I was crushed when the Children's Center in Baltimore had to close. We were running a really excellent program, but without consistent funding, there was no way to keep it going. With the money that Eddie left as well as this enormous house, I believe we could create something that would truly last."

Charlie began reimagining the space around him, trying to see it as she did. "What age group?"

"Well, my specialty is pre-school and I think that early intervention programs are still the key to making a real difference in the lives of special needs populations."

He nodded and rubbed his hand over his head. As the silence lengthened, Carolyn grew anxious. Charlie rose and walked around the perimeter of the room, touching a book or two here and there.

"Have I over-stepped here? I know this was Eddie's home and it's rude of me to think about turning it into something else when I've only just arrived. Do you think he'd be offended?"

Charlie turned and faced Carolyn with a wide grin. "I think it's an amazing idea, Carolyn, one that Eddie would have embraced wholeheartedly. You've a steep road ahead, though, with zoning laws, neighborhood groups, all kinds of people will probably come out to try and stop you."

"That's why I need you, Charlie, to help guide me. So what do you say, can I hire you as a consultant?"

"Why not?"

Carolyn stood and shook his hand. "You won't regret it, I promise." She almost shimmered with anticipation and Charlie, in turn, felt younger than he had in years.

"Where do we start?" he asked as they returned to their seats.

"I think the first thing we need is a name."

CHAPTER SIX

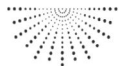

*I*t hadn't taken long for Carolyn to settle into life in Edward Clark's home. She loved the library best and had set about making the desk into her workspace. She donated things that hadn't been needed and boxed up any items she thought should be preserved before setting up her computer and files. Like any teacher, she reveled in the fresh office supplies and made the most of the enormous walnut desk. The walls were lined with classic books of all genres, but she'd managed to create an area for her education materials. Following Charlie's advice, she'd started first on writing a business plan. Using a combination of textbooks and on-line materials, she'd developed a solid outline for *The Edward Clark Children's Center* and was beginning to fill in the details when her phone rang.

She recognized her brother, Curt's number, and resigned herself to a long call. "Carolyn, you've got to help me."

"What's up, Curt. What's wrong?" She set the phone on speaker and continued to key in the numbers she'd been calculating.

"It's Mom. She's getting worse. She keeps on calling me, over and over again, with the same damn question. I've answered her four times and she won't stop." Carolyn stopped typing and leaned back in the chair.

"What question?"

"She keeps asking about Dad's ashes."

"What do you mean? They're at Arlington in the grave next to Tim."

"Well, I know that, of course. She keeps asking when we're going to the service."

Carolyn sagged back into her chair. "Wow, she doesn't remember it? I knew she was starting to forget little things, but that seems like a real change."

"Can't you go over there and check on her or something, please? She's making me crazy. I can't just leave work again to go and deal with her." His tone of voice changed. "Now that you're a millionaire, can't you just send one of your servants over or something?" That goading voice had plagued her throughout her adolescence and in that frame of mind she answered.

"Oh, grow up. I'll take care of it." She ended the call more abruptly than was polite, but then Curt was almost never polite. She doubted he'd notice. Then she dialed her mother.

"Hello?" a timid voice answered.

"Mom, it's Carolyn. How are you?"

"Carolyn, she's in Baltimore."

"No, Mom. I'm back here in Pittsburgh, remember? How are you? Would you like to come to dinner tonight? Do you have plans?"

"Plans? I didn't make any plans, was I supposed to?" Carolyn was surprised at the frightened tone in her mother's voice.

"Mom, you don't have to plan anything. Can I send a car for you around five?"

"Well, I suppose that would be all right. Can I bring something?"

"No, there's no need. I'll see you this evening. Bye now!"

"Oh, Okay, good bye."

She didn't sound good, Carolyn had to give Curt that. But he was always so prone to exaggeration. It was hard to take him seriously. She got up from the desk and went in search of Helen and plans for dinner.

Rather than ask Rupert to bring her mother, Carolyn opted to drive over herself. PJ was happily digging with Rusty in Helen's vegetable garden so it was easy to get away. The drive out to Butler didn't take long, but Carolyn was surprised at how reluctant she was to pull into the familiar driveway. Wasn't this her home? Shouldn't she feel comfortable? But she didn't. Her mother and father had bought the house in happy anticipation of her father's retirement. They had begun decorating, but her brother Tim's death left nearly everything in flux and when her father passed away, just months before returning from his last assignment, her mother collapsed.

Curt left the military for a higher paying job in the public sector and the two of them had paid a decorator to come in and finish. No one, though, had ever really felt like the house was home. Carolyn rang the doorbell and waited, not sure whether walking in was the thing to do. After a few minutes with no response, she took the unfamiliar key out of her purse and let herself in.

"Mom?" she called as she walked down the hallway. She passed the little used living room and headed toward the great room at the back of the house. There she discovered her mother pulling several small containers out of the refrigerator. "Mom, how are you?"

Carolyn stepped around the large kitchen island toward her mother.

"Oh, my Lord." Startled, her mother dropped the container as the refrigerator door banged open. "You just about scared me to death, Carolyn." Her thin hand plucked at the collar of her carefully tailored shirt.

"I rang the bell, Mom, didn't you hear it? I came to take you to dinner, remember?"

Angela looked at Carolyn's face before setting the food down and closing the heavy door. "Oh, was that tonight? I wasn't sure." `

Carolyn wanted to point out that she'd called just an hour ago, but decided that it wouldn't help the situation. "Let me just change my clothes."

Carolyn looked at the small, trim woman in the beautifully tailored clothing. The short cap of gray hair that used to always be permed into an elaborate style now boasted a no-fuss look that she was slowly getting used to.

"Mom, we're just eating at the house, you look very nice already."

Angela brushed her hand down the front of her soft, white slacks and looked up uncertainly. "Are you sure?"

"PJ is home and he's been digging in the dirt for an hour. If you'd like to put on some less-nice clothes," Carolyn laughed, "that would be fine, but you certainly don't need any that are fancier."

"Well, if you're sure. Let me just use the bathroom and collect my purse, I'll be right with you." Carolyn watched her mother move rather slowly back toward the bedroom. She took a minute to wipe up the counter and resettle the lid firmly on the container, before putting it back into the refrigerator. She paused a moment to look at the shelves. They were nearly empty, a few jars of jam and one of mayonnaise, an unopened container of coffee creamer but little else. There was no produce or anything that looked the least bit fresh. Then she opened the freezer compartment and found it nearly filled with a rather limited variety of frozen dinners. Angela had never liked cooking, but she'd always had more on hand than this.

Carolyn closed everything up and stepped into the larger room to wait. When more than five minutes had passed without her mother re-emerging, she became concerned once more. She moved down the hallway toward the bedroom, calling ahead of her.

"Mom? Everything all right?"

`Her mother was sitting on the wide bed, looking rather small, with a different shoe in each hand. She looked up at Carolyn clearly puzzled.

"I can't seem to make up my mind about which ones to wear." One was a canvas tennis shoe style while the other was a much dressier sling back. Carolyn took the dressier shoe and swapped it for the mate to the canvas one before sitting down on the bed beside her. "These are perfect, Mom. Do you need any help getting them on?"

"Well, don't be ridiculous," her mother snapped, using a harsher tone than Carolyn was expecting. Feeling hurt, she watched as her mother slipped on one shoe and then the other, before standing up. When she looked at her mother more closely though, the expression she saw wasn't anger. It looked more confused, even frightened, so she held her tongue and walked quietly with her out to the car.

Angela had little to say on the drive so Carolyn found herself lost in thought. Her relationship with her mother had had an edge to it for as long as she could remember. She knew that when she was very little Angela had delighted in dressing her up in pretty clothes and Carolyn had loved showing off for all of her mother's friends at the Officers' Club on base. Once Carolyn reached middle school though, the relationship started to change. She was no longer willing to put on the kind of outfits that her mother continued to buy, nor did she feel like accompanying her to the club. Angela didn't seem to be able to let go of the little girl that she'd been. Over time, with her father often working late, or traveling for months on end, Angela had found herself more and more alone and, looking back, Carolyn could see how her depression worsened in that isolation.

As usual, what came to mind as she reflected back on their relationship, were the two really big fights that remained locked in Carolyn's memory. The first one came during her junior year in high school when Angela found out that Carolyn had met with the Army recruiter. Although she was adopted, Carolyn was proud of her military family and she wanted to serve the way her father and brothers did. But first her mother and, then her father, had absolutely forbidden it and without their permission she was unable to sign the commitment letter. She could have made a stand when she turned 18, but by then she had begun to focus on college instead.

The second fight had occurred when she was in her sophomore year of college and planning a study year abroad. She was eager to see the world on her own and had chosen a program in South America in part for the sheer distance from home. This time, her father had played the heavy, but her mother was at his side, nodding as he made the pronouncement against her going. With their hands firmly on the purse strings, she'd had no choice but to comply. From the perspective that time had given her now, she could see the contradictory nature of their concerns. They kept saying that she wasn't ready for solo adventures, not fit for the physical challenges of the military, but at the same time they emphasized how much she was needed at home. Clearly, in their minds, she was old enough to look after her mother, but not old enough to stand on her own. It rankled still and she found herself shifting uncomfortably in her seat, trying to push aside those old complaints.

As they drew closer, her mind returned to the present and a new worry. Although Angela and her brother, Curt, knew all about the inheritance, this was the first time anyone from Carolyn's family would be seeing the house and she was feeling self-conscious. As they pulled around the large circular drive, Carolyn saw a different, almost blank look on her mother's face.

"Where are we?" she asked as Carolyn put the car into park.

"This is Edward Clark's house, Mom, PJ's great-great uncle's house. This is where I live now." Her mother's hands rested on the seatbelt strap but she made no move to unbuckle it. Finally, she turned to look at Carolyn.

"You live here? Do you work for the family or something?"

Carolyn reached over and unfastened the belt, gently easing it off her shoulder.

"Mom, PJ and I own this. It was a gift from my biological uncle before he died. Come on, let's see PJ. He'll be excited to see you." Angela opened the door and shifted to step out but the baffled look on her face remained. Carolyn took her arm and led her up the wide walk. Rupert had the door open as they stepped up. The quiet was broken by PJ's loud cry.

"Mama, Gamma!" He rushed into the foyer, his face and hands covered with dirt. Carolyn managed to stop him just short of ruining her mother's slacks. "Hey, buddy, slow down! You're a mess!"

Rusty appeared just behind him then, a trowel in each hand. Carolyn held PJ at arm's length as she smiled at both Rupert and his grandson. "Mom, this is Rupert Johns and his grandson Rusty. Everyone, this is my mother, Angela Jacobs."

Rupert graciously gave a half bow, "I'm very pleased to meet you, ma'am," before ushering Rusty and PJ ahead of him. "I'll just see what I can do to make these young men a little more presentable. Helen's just there in the kitchen if you'd like to go on in." He gestured.

Carolyn noticed then that her mother had a steel grip on the pocketbook that hung across her chest. "Let's just set this here, Mom, okay?" Carolyn asked as she eased it off over her shoulder. "I want you to come and meet Helen, Rupert's wife. She's been looking after PJ and me since we arrived."

Carolyn set the purse down before gently reaching her hand into the loop of her mother's arm and leading her forward into the kitchen. She was happy to see that Helen had set up a simple table for them in the alcove rather than using the big dining room next door. Carolyn beamed at Helen as she moved forward. "Helen, this is my mother Angela. Mom, this is Helen Johns, our chef, house mother, everything rolled into one."

Angela held out her hand and smiled. "It's so nice to meet you Mrs. Johns."

"Oh please, call me Helen. What can I get you two to drink?"

"Mom, would you like a glass of wine?"

"That would be lovely, thank you." Angela spun slowly around, taking in the massive kitchen island and double set of wall ovens before her eye caught on the enormous table in the next room. She moved on into the dining room then, running her hand along the beautiful polished wood before stepping toward the wall of windows and the view of the garden beyond. Carolyn brought her the glass of wine and moved to open the French door as her mother turned to her and asked, "How long have you been working here?"

Carolyn's hand stilled on the doorknob. She wondered then if her mother's question was a kind of slight, that somehow she didn't deserve the riches that had fallen upon her. Or maybe it was fueled by resentment, that her adopted family had not been able to provide for her the way this uncle had. She felt her familiar defenses rising but just then she looked again at her mother's face and found a return to the bewildered look she'd had when the two different shoes were in her hands. Carolyn let out a slow breath and apologized to Curt in her mind. He hadn't exaggerated. Something was really wrong.

Dr. Grace Gilbert had been her mother's doctor ever since they returned to the Pittsburgh area. Carolyn met her once before and was glad to know that there was some continuity to her mother's treatment. For so many years, they had moved from base to base, and Angela's sadness had moved with them just like the old corduroy couch. Once Carolyn had finished college and gotten her master's degree, she'd developed a better sense of what had been going. The woman who Carolyn remembered from her very early years, the one who'd laughed and sang with her, who played tea party and school with her when her brothers were just old enough to ignore her, that woman had slowly faded. It was as if each move to a new location had siphoned a small bit of her away. By nature, she was fairly shy and Carolyn thought that having to make new friends in a new community every few years, had taken a toll too.

After what felt like a fairly normal dinner, her mother often laughing at PJ's antics, Carolyn drove her home and saw her settled in. She thought that there was a sense of relief on her mother's face as she walked into her home, her hand resting briefly on the small table by the door. Carolyn wanted to stay for a few minutes, to see how her mother did getting ready for bed, but clearly Angela had had enough. She waved Carolyn away and appeared anxious to lock the door.

The next morning, Carolyn had made the appointment and driven with her mother to see Dr. Gilbert. "I'm not sure why you're here with me, Carolyn. Don't you need to get to work, to your classroom?"

"No, Mom, I have time. I just wanted to have a chance to chat with Dr. Gilbert and hear how you're doing."

Her mother drew herself up into a straighter posture and cast a disdainful glance in her direction. "This is ridiculous." She didn't quite 'harrumph,' but Carolyn thought it came close. In spite of her inherent shyness, her mother was a proud woman and Carolyn knew she needed to be careful with her approach. A few minutes later they were settled into the comfortable armchairs that faced Dr. Gilbert's desk. Carolyn wasn't surprised her mother spoke first.

"Dr. Gilbert, I'm sorry to bother you like this. Carolyn insisted."

The doctor smiled and leaned back in her seat, "I'm happy to see you as always, and I'm pleased to meet your daughter again. Tell me, Angela, how have you been feeling?"

Carolyn watched her mother slip on a practiced expression as she told Dr. Gilbert about her days. She mentioned the women's circle that she met with regularly and a fund drive at her church, but there was no mention of the dinner at Carolyn's or the calls to Curt. "Mom, can you tell Dr. Gilbert about your dinner at my house?" Carolyn waited, shifting her glance between Angela and the doctor. A pause was growing. Carolyn could see Dr. Gilbert's expression subtly change as she waited.

Angela's tone was one of exasperation. "Well, of course I haven't been to Baltimore in ages, what are you talking about?" She looked toward Dr. Gilbert for reassurance.

"Mom, this is why I'm concerned, why I asked to come with you. PJ and I live in Pittsburgh now and you came to my house for dinner on Sunday." Her mother's face was blank. Then it turned angry.

"Well, if you're talking about that, that mansion where you work, of course I remember going there."

"And I told you, I don't work there, that's my home. It was a gift from PJ's great- great uncle." Angela's anger rose again as she twisted away from Carolyn and grasped the edge of the desk.

"I'm so sorry, Dr. Gilbert, I'm sure you've dealt with many adopted children and adults before. They're just always looking for a better deal, spoiled aren't they? Never satisfied with the home they've been given." She turned her head to look back at Carolyn. "I was never enough for you, was I?"

The harsh nature of her mother's comment was as much of a surprise as was the content. Carolyn could count on one hand the number of times she and her mother had discussed her adoption. The shock must have registered on her face because the doctor quickly stepped in. "Carolyn, your mother and I have had a couple of conversations about the discovery of your biological mother. I believe it's put a bit of a strain on Angela. Have the two of you talked about it since you moved back?"

Carolyn rested her hands on the curved, wooden arms of her chair, uncertain what to say either to the doctor or her mother. She worked hard to hold her composure. "Dr. Gilbert, I'm not sure what my mother may have told you about my circumstances, but I can assure you, and her, I never went looking for my biological relatives. They found me. In fact, it turns out that my biological father is a pretty nasty criminal." She looked back at her mother. "I love my family. You're my mom and I'm worried about you. That's all. Curt and I spoke and he said you've been calling repeatedly, asking the same question over and over. It scared me so I wanted to talk with you and Dr. Gilbert to see what we can do." She rested her hands in her lap and watched as her mother's posture deflated a bit.

Angela's tone turned to one of hurt. "Well, I'm so sorry to be a worry to you and your brother. I'll just put that silly cell phone he got me away and let the two of you be."

"Mom, that's not— ," but Doctor Gilbert interrupted.

"Angela, I'm glad that Carolyn's here, that Curt called her and told her he was worried about you. You're right, I do work with many individuals who've been adopted, but what I'm seeing here isn't resentment, it's love. I think you're pretty lucky to have two children who love you enough to get involved."

But Angela's face sunk further.

"Two children and no husband, that's what's left, isn't it?"

Carolyn reached over and rested her hand gently on her mother's arm. "I miss them too, Mom, every day. That's why I don't want to lose you, too." She turned to Dr. Gilbert. "Let's be honest, Dr. Gilbert. I know my mother has depression and that working with you has made a big difference, but is there more that can be done? Could memory issues be a sign of something else?" She could sense her mother bristle at the word depression, but Angela continued to sit quietly.

Dr. Gilbert leaned forward. Her short, white hair caught the sunlight coming in the window as she lifted a folder and set it aside. "I agree, memory issues could be a real concern Angela and there's testing we can do to look at that, but I don't want to jump to any conclusions here. I will tell you both, though, that a key factor working against you Angela, is how isolated you've become. At this point, I think that's my chief concern."

Angela stiffened. "What do you mean? I drive, I get out, I'm not some sort of shut-in."

"Mom, how often do you leave your house?" Carolyn tried to ask with a gentle tone. "Once, maybe twice a week?"

Her mother looked at Dr. Gilbert.

"She's right, Angela, that's not enough." Carolyn watched the exchange and thought of how their roles had changed so much in the last year. She had so many resources now, surely there was more she could do.

"Dr. Gilbert, I would like to look into the testing you mentioned." She could sense her mother shifting uncomfortably so she turned to her and tried to use a calm voice. "Mom, I'm working to open a children's center at the house. I wonder if you might be willing to come and stay with PJ one or two mornings a week. He would love to see you and it would give me some quiet time to work."

Angela looked up then, and smiled unexpectedly. "He's a sweet, sweet boy, I would love to see him."

"I think that's an excellent idea." Dr. Gilbert rose and came around to the front of the desk. "Angela, would you be willing to do some testing, to look at the memory questions we have?"

Angela paused but then straightened in her seat, "Yes, I think it's just like anyone else though, forgetting where they left their keys or such, but I can do the testing."

"Great," Dr. Gilbert responded. "Would you step out and talk with Sheila about getting that on our schedule? You can let her know about any prescriptions you need refilled too."

Angela stood, looked at Carolyn and turned away before leaving the office. Carolyn stood then also, her hand in the air where she had reached out toward her mother. She dropped it back to her side and started to leave but Dr. Gilbert gestured her back into her seat and took Angela's chair beside her. "I'm glad you brought her in today. I'm curious, what is the question that she keeps calling your brother about?"

Carolyn sat down, twisting the strap to her purse as she spoke. "She keeps asking him about our dad's ashes and when the service is. It's hard on him. He left the military right after Tim died, you know and I think our last visit to Arlington was even harder for him than it was for Mom."

"Survivor's guilt maybe?" Carolyn shrugged.

"I don't know. It's a little more complicated than that." Carolyn shrugged self-consciously. "Tim was really mom's favorite. We didn't talk about it much but it was always there. Curt knows he'll never be enough, we'll," she pointed to herself, "we'll never be enough. What do you think is going on, really?"

"Well, unfortunately, early on-set dementia can appear in patients who have a history of clinical depression. I'm not saying that's what's happening here, just that it's a possibility. I was being honest when I said that I think your mother's social isolation is a real issue. Having her over to spend time with your son sounds like a wonderful start." She smiled. "Now tell me about this children's center." Her eyes twinkled, "I remember the inheritance you received and I'd love to know what it is you're planning!"

CHAPTER SEVEN

*L*abor Day. Carolyn couldn't remember the last time the holiday hadn't been filled with school preparations, but she did have to give herself a small pat on the back. Charlie and the lawyers had finally approved her business plan and her fight with the neighborhood association seemed to be working out as well. The estate's position at the back of the development had helped and she had agreed to put in a secondary access road straight to the property so that her clients would have a direct route in and out without disturbing the other homeowners. In fact, one member of the association was ready to enroll their preschooler. That felt like an even bigger achievement.

Now, though, it was a holiday. Her mother and Curt were both on their way over for a cookout, so she closed her laptop and put away work thoughts. PJ came running up just as she closed the door to the library. "She's here, Mommy!" She scooped him up in her arms and they made their way to the foyer where Rupert was already reaching for the doorknob. She was pleased to see her mother looking so well. She had on a beautiful flowered shirt with pale blue slacks but more importantly, she wore a smile.

"Let me take that for you, Mom." Carolyn put PJ down and

leaned in to give her mother a quick kiss on the cheek before taking a container of deviled eggs. Then Angela bent down to PJ's level and gave him a hug.

"How are you doing little one?"

Carolyn could see Rupert smiling as he closed the door and the four of them moved together toward the kitchen. "Something smells delicious!" Helen emerged from around the refrigerator and beamed at Angela.

"Thank you! Can't beat a pan of warm brownies for brightening up a kitchen!"

"Bownies! Bownies!" PJ was jumping up and down.

"After dinner, PJ," Angela admonished him but with a kind tickle, PJ was off and running toward the garden door.

"C'mon, Mom, PJ convinced us to eat outdoors so we're setting everything up out here."

Rupert and Helen followed them out with platters of food. Rusty was already out there, holding down a corner of the tablecloth.

"It keeps trying to blow away." The garden was ringed with pots of late summer asters and mums so Rupert picked up one of them to anchor the tablecloth. Rusty grinned. When they first made the plan to have her mother come and watch PJ, Carolyn worried what she would make of Rusty. She couldn't remember a single disabled child, or adult from when she was little, and she wasn't sure how her mother would react. Truth be told, Angela was a bit awkward at first, but little by little Rusty won her over. She beamed at him from across the table.

"Now that did the trick, didn't it?"

They heard the doorbell. Rupert left to answer it. He returned with Curt and a beautiful, dark haired young woman. "Hi, Carolyn. Mom, I hope it's all right that I brought Brenda."

Carolyn stepped forward. "Of course, hello, I'm Carolyn. I'm so glad you could come. Curt, this is Rupert Johns and his wife Helen and their grandson Rusty." Curt looked a bit ill at ease as he shook hands all around, but Brenda stepped up with more warmth in her greeting and soon they were all chatting around the patio table.

They had nearly finished the main part of the meal when the doorbell rang again. Rupert looked questioningly at Carolyn but she shrugged her shoulders. "I wasn't expecting anyone else, were you?" Helen shook her head as Carolyn went with Rupert to see to the door.

His tall athletic build and striking blue eyes, still had the power to make her pulse race. "I have this, Rupert." Carolyn nodded to let him know he could return to the party. He gave a quick nod in return and left. "Alex, what are you doing here?" She kept her hand on the doorknob, waiting to see what her ex-husband would say.

"Caro, it's the holiday. I came to see you and PJ, of course."

"But how did you find us?" She stood still, not allowing him to enter.

"I asked Janine and she gave me this address. Is this some kind of school? How long have you been working here?"

"It will be a school. It's just getting started at this point."

"Well, can I come in? Will they mind?"

Carolyn paused as PJ came running to the door.

"Daddy!" he yelled and Alex scooped him up in his arms.

"Wow, you're so big!" He hefted him in his arms, grinning, just as PJ started wiggling to get down.

"Come on. It's picnic outside!" PJ began pulling his father along the entryway. Carolyn had no choice but to follow. When they got to the back garden, Curt was the first to step forward.

"Alex, how are you? I haven't seen you in forever!" He and Alex did the man hug, pounding each other on the shoulder before stepping back.

"I'm good, I'm good. How are you?" He turned to her mother then, "Angela, you look well. No, no, don't get up. Everyone, sit down, I didn't mean to interrupt."

Rupert brought another wrought iron chair over to the table while Helen went to get an extra plate. PJ was happily sitting on Alex's knee as Carolyn stood stiffly to the side. She'd never told her mother, or Curt, what had finally pushed her to leave the marriage. Only Janine, her best friend back in Baltimore, had been there through it all with her. How many times during PJ's first year, had she found herself crying her eyes out at Janine's kitchen table? It had been that way since PJ's birth.

"He's a firefighter, Janine. Nothing I do, even my work at school, can compare with that. It's not just his job, it's his calling. He saves peoples' lives and all I can do is whine that he's never home."

"Well, he's not home, that's a fact. I don't remember seeing his ass when you and I were at the ER last weekend with PJ, did you?" Janine handed Carolyn another tissue. "It's noble work, but so is being a teacher, being a mother. You can't keep comparing yourself to him. It's not fair to you or PJ." She paused and looked at her friend, the tears still falling onto the cluttered table. Her voice grew quiet. "There's something else, isn't there?"

Carolyn threw the crumpled tissue onto the table, then stood and picked up the whole pile to throw away. Her eyes were drier but her face looked sadder when she sat back down across from Janine. "Yeah, there's something else. He kept talking about this other firefighter, Chris this and Chris that, how great they were. Then one night he came in smelling like some kind of lemon shampoo." She turned to face her friend. "It had never occurred to me that Chris was a woman, someone he claimed understood him better." She and Janine talked on into the night, PJ asleep in the playpen, both of them growing angrier as the night went on. Near dawn Janine happened to mention an apartment she'd heard was available down the street. The next day, Carolyn rented the apartment and moved her and PJ out while Alex was on an extended shift. As she stood there in the garden now, she had to

48

admit, after that neither of them put up much of a fight to save the marriage.

Curt was laughing at some sports joke with Alex when he turned and looked at Carolyn. "So what's Alex think about the new..." He spread his hands wide gesturing at their surroundings when she shook her head.

"The new school? I haven't told him much about it." She looked at Curt, clear that he'd gotten her signal, then turned back to Alex and began telling him about the program. Once she felt his interest lagging, she stopped, lured PJ over with a toy car and then sent him off to play under Rusty's careful eye. "So, Alex, why are you in Pittsburgh?"

"Actually, I wanted to talk to you about that. Could we?" He crumpled the napkin and set it on the table and nodded back toward the house.

"Certainly, will you all excuse us?" She led him back inside to the library where she settled herself behind the big desk. She felt she needed the home court advantage. He sat across from her in the leather armchair.

"Wow, you sure make yourself at home. How'd you even find this job?"

"Alex, why are you here?" She kept her hands clenched in her lap, waiting for his response. He scrubbed his hands through his dark hair before looking up again, but in that moment she saw a wide, angry scar on the edge of his long sleeve. "Are you hurt, Alex?" Carolyn gestured at his arm, but he quickly pulled his sleeve down further.

"It's nothing. That's not why I'm here."

Carolyn waited, her knuckles growing white.

"There was this fire."

Carolyn shifted in her seat, tucking her hands under her legs as she waited for the familiar story. "Of course."

"No, you don't understand. This was different." He paused and then stood, walking toward one of the walls of books. He rested his hand on the tall ladder before turning to face her. "It all went wrong, from the very beginning. It was an old, abandoned building but we were told there were squatters inside, a group with kids in it, someone said. Juan led a team of us in but we couldn't find anyone on the first floor. It was starting to get really bad, when I thought I heard something. I pointed up the stairs and Juan and Chris took off ahead of me." He sat down on the steps of the ladder, his hands spread wide on his knees, then plucking at the seam of his jeans.

"When the beam fell, it hit Juan first. We could tell he was gone right away but Chris didn't want to give up. We pulled and pulled on the beam until we could get it off him, just as a second one gave way. It laid Chris's leg open, bad. I had no choice. I had to leave Juan behind and get Chris out to safety. Once I had her out, I started back inside for him but the chief wouldn't let me. Christ." He shook his head. "It was like nothing I'd ever seen. The whole structure ended up caving in. In the end, the only body we found inside was Juan's." He paused as he rubbed his hands back and forth over his knees.

Carolyn's voice was soft. "What happened after that?"

Alex looked up, then stood and walked back to the chair. "I'm not sure. Chris ended up in physical therapy for a long time. She may never walk without a cane." He crossed his leg, resting one foot on the other knee. "The joke was on me when she fell for her physical therapist."

Carolyn looked down at the edges of the desk drawer, trying to keep her focus as she thought about what he was saying. Then she looked up at the familiar face and wondered how much had really changed. "So, why are you in Pittsburgh, Alex? What's going on?"

"Carolyn, I miss you, I miss PJ—our family."

"Our family was just me and PJ, Alex. You were never home

enough to be a part of a family. Why should I listen to you now? Because Chris is unavailable? Is that why you're here?"

"No, shit no, that has nothing to do with it." He stood up abruptly. "Caro, listen, after that fire, I had to think, to really think. Juan was only five years older than me. He had a wife and two kids and now they're all alone. He was a good family man, too, put them first whenever he could and look what happened." He paced back and forth between the chair and the shelves. "It made me realize Carolyn, what I'd lost, what I'd thrown away really. I love fighting fires, I think it's what I was born to do, but I realize now it's not the only thing I was born to do." He sat back down. "Don't be mad at me, I went to see Janine. She told me you'd been seeing her brother Sean but that it had ended when you moved here. So, I did some job hunting in the area. There's a firefighting academy just south of here. I've got an interview tomorrow to be an instructor there."

"So you thought you'd just show up here, that everything would be okay? It's not that easy, Alex. A lot has changed for you, I hear that, but a lot has changed for me too."

"I know, Caro, I know. This job for one, looks amazing. I just want to know if I can see you again, if I can see PJ. Please?" He rested his hands on the back of the big chair. "Carolyn, I gave up too easily before. Please, let me have another chance."

Carolyn stood and walked to the door, trying her best to look calm while everything inside her was going crazy. "You have to go now, I'm sorry. This is just too much. Call me later this week, after your interview is over and you know what you're going to do. I have to think about all of this. I'll walk you out back so that you can say goodbye to PJ, but then you have to leave."

"Fair enough. I appreciate you listening at least."

There were a lot of curious faces when they returned to the garden, but PJ ran up first and Alex swung him into a big hug. "I have to go now, buddy. I'll see you soon."

"Okay, Daddy." He suffered one more hug before squirming to get down.

Helen was using sidewalk chalk to show PJ and Rusty how to play hopscotch on the wide slate patio. Alex surveyed the group scattered around the garden, nodded at Curt, and then left. Curt waited until he was sure he was gone.

"What the hell, Carolyn? He doesn't know about the inheritance, about all of this?" He gestured around him at the house and grounds.

Not wanting to talk about it further, she simply shook her head.

"Did I miss out on the brownies?" she called to PJ who dropped the chalk and came running.

CHAPTER EIGHT

The next few weeks went quickly for Carolyn. Alex had gotten the job as instructor and returned to Baltimore to collect his things. In the meantime, construction had begun on the access road and it was all Helen and Rupert could do to keep PJ and Rusty away from the equipment. They could stand for hours, it seemed, watching the big machines clearing and paving. On the day the crew was finally painting the stripes, they all took a walk down the new road to where it met the larger street.

"Looks like you're underway now, Miss." Rupert smiled.

Carolyn grinned and swung PJ around in a quick dance. "That we are. I can't wait! I've made great progress getting the atrium ready and the furniture is supposed to be delivered on Monday." She spread her arms wide. "And now they have a brand new road to bring it in on!"

Once she had settled back down at her desk, Carolyn wrote out the final payment to the paving company and then began checking up on her other orders. When the phone rang, she was pleased to see that it was Dr. Gilbert. "Good afternoon, Dr. Gilbert."

"Call me Grace, won't you?"

Carolyn smiled as she entered the most recent figures into her spreadsheet. "What can I do for you, Grace? Oh, I can't thank you enough for sending Susan to me. I can't wait to begin working with her. She's had so many good ideas about the set up already!"

Dr. Susan Gilbert was her mother's daughter in many ways. Her short blonde hair was so light it reminded Carolyn of Grace's white hair, but although she was also tall, Susan was definitely curvy where her mother was lean and angular. She'd followed her mother into the field of psychology but had specialized in pediatrics. Together, Susan and Carolyn had made a plan for the testing and conference space that would allow for a one-way mirror and viewing area into the classroom. Even now the glass was being installed.

"I'm so pleased it's working out. I know Susan's especially happy to be getting out of the office regularly. But, I'm afraid that's not why I called. I wanted to talk with you about the test results for your mother."

"More tests? I thought she was doing better. She's been coming three times a week to stay with PJ and she seems okay."

"Well, I did some tests with her after you brought her in originally and I do think the medication changes we made have helped. But I have to be honest with you. I repeated some of the simpler ones with her at our session today and there was a marked difference. It was clear that she didn't remember having done them before. She also told me something alarming, which I don't think she shared with you. Last week, she had a small fire."

"WHAT?" Carolyn stood quickly, the spreadsheets forgotten.

"It's okay. She told me that she left a pot of water boiling on the stove and came back to find the pot black and smoldering. It didn't catch onto anything else and she did handle the situation correctly, but you can see why I'd be concerned."

Carolyn fell back into her chair. "I don't understand though, Grace. My mother's only 65. Isn't she too young for this sort of thing?"

"You're right, she is younger than the patients we typically see with dementia. But, unfortunately, sometimes we see depression morph into dementia and senility as the patient ages. I suspect that's what's happening."

Angela's life had already been limited by the struggles she'd faced with depression. It didn't seem fair that life was getting harder now that she was growing older. "I have to do something more, don't I?"

There was a pause before Grace answered. "I'm afraid I think you do, Carolyn. I'm really fond of Angela, after all these years. I'd hate for something to happen to her. The other thing that she mentioned to me is that she's having some trouble driving places. I think she frightened herself last week when she got lost on her way to your place."

"I wish she'd said something to me."

"Well, it's a hard thing to admit, Carolyn, for anyone. If you want my help finding some care for her, or a facility of some kind, please let me know."

Carolyn finished the conversation somehow, but didn't really remember much after the mention of a facility. She couldn't put her mother away. How could she do that? Angela was coming that afternoon to see PJ, she'd have to think of something by then. She turned back to her email in an effort to get a bit more work done but there was no comfort there. The first entry was from Charlie with the subject line *STOP EVERYTHING*. That was followed by the sound of breaking glass. What now?

She ran from the office and followed the noise to the back of the atrium where the thousand-dollar piece of mirrored glass was now a pile of shards scattered in a huge radius. The workman's assistant, a young man in a dirty ball cap, was busy trying to sweep it up at the same time his boss was screaming at him. Carolyn entered the room and held up her hand for the man to stop. He quieted abruptly and elbowed the assistant.

Carolyn asked, "What's going on?" Just as she spotted a worn basketball, she heard a small voice and a deeper one, crying in the next room. The workman and his assistant both looked at her, then the younger man handed her the ball and started the Shopvac to continue the cleanup.

Carolyn paused and knocked her feet against the doorjamb to be sure that she wasn't tracking the pieces around and to give herself a moment to think. Then she turned the corner into the next room where Rusty and PJ were both sitting in the middle of the empty room, sobbing. She saw Rupert across the hall but indicated to him that she would handle it. She had to scold them but first she had to make sure they were safe. She sat down on the floor between them and was reassured that there was no blood.

"All right guys, tell me what happened." The wails grew louder. She looked at Rusty. "Are either of you hurt?"

Rusty dried his tears on his shirtsleeves and managed to get some control. He took two big gulps of air. "We're not hurt, Miss Carolyn. It was an accident."

"What kind of accident, Rusty?"

"PJ threw the basketball really well and I missed it."

"You were playing in here? Inside?" PJ and Rusty shared a look before each nodded. "Do you see why it's not allowed? Both of you could have gotten really hurt. That's why balls are supposed to stay outside."

Rusty spoke up. "You have to punish us. We could help clean up."

Carolyn nodded. "That's nice of you to offer, but it's not safe." She caught Rupert's eye. "Rupert, is there some cleaning up that needs to be done somewhere else in the house?"

He nodded, approving of her plan. "Certainly, there's always cleaning to do." He took a stern tone. "Gentlemen." The three of them rose and Rupert gave Carolyn a quick wink before ushering the two of them out. Then the workman came in.

"Uh, Miss, I'm going to have to special order another one, probably take a week at least."

"All right, thank you for your help. I'm sorry this happened. Wait." She remembered the subject heading of Charlie's email. "Uh, for now, can you just continue on the other work that's been started? I'll take care of ordering the glass." He nodded and ducked his head before returning to the clean-up.

Back at her desk Carolyn opened the email from Charlie. The text said:

The lawyers have just told me that there is a question about Eddie's estate. Jay Warren's uncle James is challenging the settlement on his behalf. He's got some money and a team of top-notch lawyers. Our guys don't think he can make anything stick, but they're urging us to be cautious with our spending. Sorry to be the bearer of bad tidings. I'll let you know more as soon as I can.

Carolyn dropped her head into her hands. What would she do? She'd spent so much already, the road, the furniture and now she needed another thousand-dollar mirror. She closed her laptop and walked away, not sure what step to take. Then she heard the door. Helen was a step ahead of her, just letting Angela in as Carolyn arrived.

"Let me take your coat, Angela," Helen offered. For a half second, Carolyn could see the pause in her mother's movements, as if she were uncertain what had been said. Carolyn reached to help her ease out of the coat and she began moving once again.

"How was your drive, Mom?" Carolyn led her toward the kitchen area.

"Fine, it was fine. Of course. Why are you asking?" She looked at Carolyn with distrust.

Once they were in the kitchen, Carolyn offered her a bar stool and sat down beside her. "Helen made some cookies this morning. Would you like one?" The look of distrust was slowly replaced with a smile.

"They smell wonderful."

Carolyn smiled. "I have to tell you, PJ's in the doghouse right now. He and Rusty managed to break a really expensive mirror."

"They weren't hurt were they?"

"No, they're fine. Oh thank you, Helen." Helen offered them both a cup of tea and Angela seemed to relax just a bit more. She was chatting with them when PJ and Rusty came into view.

"Cookies," they both yelled and Angela quieted them with a harsh look and tone that Carolyn was all too familiar with.

"Really, that is not the way that young men come into a room," she barked.

Both Rusty and PJ looked up frightened before sitting down silently at the small table nearby.

Carolyn took a kinder tone. "Have you two finished your work for Rupert?" They both nodded and Helen brought over two glasses of milk and the platter of cookies. "All right, have a snack and then Grandma can read you some stories, PJ." He nodded and sipped noisily on his cup. Carolyn turned to Angela. "Mom, will you read with PJ when he's done? He can show you where his favorite books are. Then, I'd love it if you'd stay for dinner with us."

Angela looked around at the large kitchen and nodded yes, and once he'd finished, headed with PJ down the hall to his room. Once they'd gone, Rusty followed after Rupert and Helen came to sit on the next stool. "Tough morning was it?"

"Oh, Helen, you have no idea. That glass that the boys broke, cost over a thousand dollars. Charlie just sent an email saying that the estate is being challenged and Mom's doctor says she's reached a stage where she needs a lot more care. What am I going to do?"

Helen patted her on the hand and then moved the cookie plate closer. "First things first. There's not much that can't be improved by a warm, molasses cookie." She smiled as Carolyn took a good bite. "This place is your home now. Nothing's going to change that.

I don't care what a bunch of lawyers say. Just keep doing what you're doing and let it all work itself out."

"Are you always this optimistic, Helen, or is it the cookies?" Carolyn laughed.

"Well, a cookie now and then can't hurt." She got up and began clearing the glasses before turning back to Carolyn. "Why don't you have your mother come and stay here with us?"

"Here? Are you serious? Did you hear her just now?" Carolyn shook her head back and forth. "I know she's seemed okay recently but that tone just now, with the boys? I remember that tone. When she's not on her best behavior, my mother is very difficult. She's been depressed as long as I can remember and, it's gotten worse. I'm not sure I could live with that again."

Helen wrapped her arm around Carolyn's shoulders and gave her a squeeze. "It's a pretty big house, you know. I think we could find a way to share it with her, if she'll have it."

Carolyn looked up. "That's another question, isn't it? If she'll have it. Geez, does it ever get any easier?"

Helen's face took on a somber cast. "My experience is that it gets harder and then they're gone. Let's just start with dinner. Maybe she'd like to stay the night then, it's starting to get dark so much earlier.

Carolyn smiled. "Thank you, Helen. You are the calm in the middle of the storm. "

"Oh, it's such a pleasure to have this house full of people again. I'll just go and fix up the bedroom next to yours for her."

Carolyn picked up a second cookie and turned to go. It was time to call Curt and start to figure out their next steps.

CHAPTER NINE

*I*t didn't take a genius to recognize that the two enormous men hunched over the tiny kitchen table were brothers. With similar postures and nearly matching T-shirts, three-day beards and identical hooked noses, the Morelli brothers could be nothing else. Bottles and empty chip bags were scattered around the edges of the table and leading across the floor toward the overstuffed trashcan. Pizza boxes leaned against the cabinet, a line of ants snaking from one box around and out the door. A stink made up of stale coffee, burnt eggs and beer hung in the room.

"Fucking cards." Tony slammed his poker hand on to the table. "How much longer are we supposed to wait in this goddamned hell hole?" His surprisingly high, tenor voice grated on Vince's nerves, and he slammed his hand on the table as well.

"Can't you just shut the fuck up and play cards? The rules are 'go to the safe house and wait'. What part of that is so hard to understand?"

Tony slammed his chair back and rose to pace the tiny room. "What makes you so sure someone's coming? Walt's dead and his son, that rat-bastard Jay, is in jail. Who the fuck do you think we're waiting for?"

Vince was getting ready to stand and confront his brother further, when a crash sounded on the street below them setting off a neighborhood dog. Moving as one, they reached for their pistols and positioned themselves on either side of the kitchen door. Minutes later, they braced as a key slid easily into the lock and the doorknob turned.

"Tony, you here?" Pete Turner had his own gun out and led with that as he made his way into the room. He spotted Tony to his right, but kept his weapon level as he entered. Pete was 20 years older and at least a foot shorter than the muscleman, but once inside he lowered his weapon.

At that moment, his eye caught movement on the other side of the door where Vince was standing rigid, his face ashen and his gun hand shaking.

"Pete?" he sputtered out, "I thought you..."

"You thought I was dead, didn't you, you fucking bastard." Pete shrugged his shoulders and feigned a lunge toward Vince's cowering figure, before standing back upright and holstering his weapon. "Damn, you guys live like pigs."

Tony cleared a space on the table and offered his chair to the older man. Pete closed the door behind him and moved toward the seat. He gestured at Vince, who stood rooted in the corner, "Sit down, you idiot. I know you were only following orders."

"Jay told me to take out you and Al as we were leaving. I hated like hell to have to do it, you gotta know that," Vince sputtered before moving forward into the room.

"Aw, fuck it, who cares? We're all Jay's trash at this point."

Tony sat down across from the older man and collected the cards back into a neat deck. "What do you mean trash, Pete? We've been holed up here for more than a month. What gives?" Pete leaned back away from the filthy table while the big man leaned in.

"You tell me. It's taken me all this time just to get back from fucking Venezuela after Vince the moron here torched my car. It's the other goddamned side of the planet." Vince retrieved a folding chair from the next room and moved to join the other two at the table. "What's been going on here?"

Vince and Tony looked at each other before turning back to face Pete. "Uh, nothing really." Tony gestured toward the garbage. "A lot of fast food. Want a beer?" He gestured to Vince who quickly grabbed a beer from the nearly empty refrigerator and set it down in front of the older man.

"What do you mean nothing? What's the last thing you idiots did?"

The big men looked at each other before Tony finally spoke. "Well, after Jay left the warehouse, I cleaned everything up and went home like he told me. But then I heard on the news about the shooting at the restaurant so I came back here. I called up Vince and he met me here."

"Wait, back up. The last thing I did here in the spring, was take out the accountant, Arnie Lowe."

"That was nice work, Pete," Vince added. "Cops never found out a thing about that hit, no charges, nothing."

Pete nodded. "So, what happened after that, after Vince and I left to meet Jay in Caracas?"

Tony raked a meaty hand through his thinning hair, leaving the ends sticking up above his ears. He leaned forward and continued his story. "Well, once you guys were ready to come back, Jay had me check up on Clark, his uncle. Hanes had told him that Clark was at his home over in the Hartwood Manor neighborhood so I went over there. Turned out, his car was there but Clark was gone. He'd left for Baltimore with his old codger buddy. Jay said, get to Baltimore and pick up Hanes. He was that pissed."

Pete stood and walked away from the dirty table, then leaned against the kitchen counter. He took a swig of the beer. "So what'd you do then?"

Tony finished his beer and crushed the can before tossing it against the growing trash pile. "I went to fucking Baltimore, found Hanes and took him down to this warehouse."

"What warehouse? What are you talking about?"

Tony looked up, a grin on his wide face. "It was sweet, this old warehouse down by the docks. Reminded me of that one where the women were coming in down in Philly." He leaned back in the small kitchen chair. It complained loudly but held together as the big man shifted.

"So what'd you do with Hanes's body?"

Tony looked up quickly, shaking his head. "I hate that guy. He gives me the creeps." Tony shuddered. "I beat the hell out of him but I didn't kill him. Jay took him with him to that restaurant."

Pete barked out a laugh. "What? You think cause, he's queer he's gonna want you? Get over yourself. So where are the feds holding him? He's a loose thread we need to tie up fast."

Again, Tony looked at his brother before responding. "The feds don't have him."

"How do you know?"

This time Tony sounded more certain. "Jay's lawyer called to check on us one time. He told us."

"What do you mean? Where is he then?"

Both big men shrugged but neither spoke. Pete looked from one to the other before focusing back on Tony. "Unbelievable. So, you have no idea where Hanes is, you heard from James?"

"James?" Tony asked but both men looked puzzled. "The guy who runs the numbers? Why would he contact us?"

"Uh, because he's Walt Warren's brother and probably the one in charge of everything now."

Tony stood up and moved to get another beer. "That's his brother? You mean the big fat guy, the one who never moves?"

"Yeah, great big gut, white hair, that's Walt's younger brother. They were tight."

Vince shook his head when Tony offered him another. "Jay was always making fun of the guy. We never took him seriously."

"Well, I think you'd better start." Pete pulled a battered old flip phone out of his pocket and dialed as Vince and Tony exchanged glances.

CHAPTER TEN

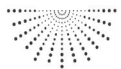

*R*ay tossed the creased newspaper into the recycle bin and moved back toward his desk. The room was humming with the work of many agents, but Ray was focused on just one. Cindy O'Brien was one of the FBI's top computer analysts and the best he'd ever worked with. She was also the most beautiful and, at the moment, she was leaning over his desk, spinning a pen as she listened to the message playing back on his desk phone. It was garbled, but she was able to make out most of it.

"*(static)Gregory Hanes... urgent care...Dr. Ling, set a broken arm, treated a concussion...not hospitalized. Said he'd been beaten over an unpaid debt, drove away under his own steam before six PM... (static) no make on the car.*

While she was listening, Ray moved closer and couldn't help but notice as she tucked the dark curls behind her ear. He wanted to reach up and do it for her, but this was work and small pleasures like that would have to wait. He smiled at her instead and as the recording finished, he gestured toward the empty seat by his desk. "Have you been able to trace anything beyond that message?" he asked.

"Not much. I just wanted to listen one more time. I think it was a fluke that he used his real name at the urgent care center, perhaps he was too out of it. Everyone's description was that the beating he took was serious. In fact, the first thing he did at the center was black out. I talked with the doctor who treated him and she indicated that another patient had spotted him in the parking lot vomiting before he passed out in his car. She was shocked that he'd been able to drive at all. After the doctor patched him up, she really wanted to have him admitted to the hospital nearby, but he wouldn't hear of it, cited money as the reason." She looked at Ray and settled into his visitor's chair. "We had the vague sense that he was going to continue south, so I've been continuing to monitor his accounts. There was an ATM withdrawal yesterday that I was able to track to a crummy neighborhood in Richmond, VA. I got a local agent to check out the area but he came up empty." She shrugged. "Do we know anything about ties he might have in that part of the country?"

Ray shook his head just as the phone rang. "Agent Sanchez."

"Detective, I'm sorry to keep pestering you. I wanted to call and ask again if you've heard anything about my friend, Greg."

"Not yet, Marybeth. I'm sorry. Have you thought of any places where he might go to hide?"

"No, I'm afraid I just don't know him that well. We were friends in high school but that's so long ago now. I wish I could help."

"Well, call us if you think of anything. We'll keep you posted." He hung up and turned back to Cindy. "She's called a few times already. She's frustrated he hasn't contacted her." The agent flipped open a folder. "His original application for the Pittsburgh police listed just a father, living out in Lancaster County somewhere. He passed more than a year ago so there was no follow up there. The bottom line is, Greg Hanes is in hiding. He's hiding from us and from whatever's left of the Warren organization."

"Do we know any more about what is left?" Cindy leaned on the desk beside her and Ray caught the bright, clean scent of her. He leaned in closer and moved his computer screen so that she could see better. Police photos spread across the top with two candid shots beneath.

"No one has seen either of the Morelli brothers, Tony and Vince, but neither have we had any hefty-sized dead bodies show up. Speculation is that one or the other gave Hanes the beating. We know that the accountant Jay used was killed earlier this spring." He tapped the photo of a car accident on the screen. "Another one of those hit-and-runs that seem to happen so often to people the Warrens don't care for. Arnie Lowe was his name, and I wonder what information was lost with his death."

He paused, then moved on to another, more hazy photo of an older man. "This guy, Pete Turner, mid-fifties, he's a big question mark. We're pretty sure that he was in Caracas with Jay and that he was still registered at the resort when the car bomb went off in the parking lot. The car was toast, one dead body there, still working on his ID, but it was not a match for Turner physically. What's really interesting is that there was a fire in one of the lower level bedrooms, not long after the car bomb went off. No dead bodies were found there, just a bunch of clothes and some fake ID's. I think Turner's in the wind."

Cindy looked at Ray as he resettled his Buddy Holly glasses on his nose and for a second, they both leaned the slightest bit forward. Then she continued, "Well, everyone here is focused back in the city, re-tracing the earlier allegations with Marybeth Rogers's help. I'm not sure what more we can do."

Ray stretched his hands above his head, then rapped his index fingers on the desk in impatience. "I want to find Hanes, whatever that takes."

"Why, do you want to prosecute him? I don't imagine Jay Warren gave him much of a say."

Ray shook his head. "No, no, I don't want to charge him. But, I do think he was under the Warren thumb long enough to know things, inside information that could seal up this case. Listen, I don't want just Jay Warren, I want us to bring every nasty piece of the operation out into the light. To do that, I think you and I should focus on finding, Turner and Hanes."

Cindy nodded. "Why don't I continue looking into Greg Hanes while you concentrate on Pete Turner?"

"Works for me." He leaned in closer. "Then dinner tonight, my place?" She smiled and gave a quick nod before leaving for her desk on the next floor.

That evening they managed *not* to talk about the case. It took deliberate effort but they were still at the getting-to-know-you-better stage so there was plenty else to talk about. They'd made an appointment to meet up in the morning and for the time being, they let everything else go. The evening was still warm and they took their time walking from work to Ray's apartment. Cindy stopped to point out one of the vantage points that she had used to take a photograph of the city's skyline.

"How long have you been interested in photography?" Ray asked as they continued to walk.

"I started when I was in middle school. My dad gave me a little camera for my birthday and I think he was surprised at how much I liked it. When I got to high school, I took some classes and learned how to do the developing."

"Do you have a dark room?"

Cindy laughed, "No, I could never afford one. Once I was out of high school I switched over to a digital camera. I've got a laptop at home that I've rigged out with a bunch of software for editing." She shrugged. "I guess taking the pictures gets me out of the house and working with them later gives me something to do in the evening."

Ray was nervous about the next question, after all, they knew so little about each other. "Have you been seeing anyone, I mean, before now?" He knew he'd asked it awkwardly and was afraid she'd laugh at his clumsy attempt at maneuvering the conversation around, but she smiled and looked at him shyly.

"I was married for two years back in college before I joined the FBI."

Ray stopped abruptly. "Married? Really?"

Cindy shook her head and shoved her hands down into the pockets of her jacket. They had stopped walking and the breeze around them had turned a shade cooler. "He was someone from my old neighborhood. My mom and dad really liked him, in fact, I think they're still disappointed in me for ending it."

"Why did you?"

She took her hand out of her pocket and hooked her arm through his as she leaned into him before continuing their walk. "It feels like so long ago now, it's hard to explain. We liked each other, we'd been good friends all through high school and I think part of it was just that we were both a little afraid of what going to college would be like. And at first, it was nice. Pitt was so big and it was great to have someone there with me. But, once we both got comfortable, we drifted. It was all very friendly. I still see him in the old neighborhood sometimes. He's got twins in second grade so it all worked out."

Ray paused and turned to face her. He rested his hands on her shoulders and pulled her in for a kiss. He had meant it to be brief, but it was soon clear that that would not be enough. Luckily for both of them, they'd nearly reached his building.

At eight, the next morning they settled at Cindy's desk. Ray started. "I haven't found much new about Turner, yet. I was able to confirm him in Caracas and I have a tentative ID of him in the Miami airport about a week ago. It's not for sure, but it is a place to start. My next step is to figure out if he's made it back into the city. The other thing I'm not sure of is his standing in the organization. I don't know if the people who are left, Walt's brother James Warren especially, will accept the guys Jay worked with or consider them tainted. I've got a beat cop friend of mine as well as a CI from the neighborhood keeping an eye out. I expect we're going to hear something. "

Cindy pulled up a set of photographs on her computer. "So, I began going back over the surveillance footage from this year and last."

"That must have taken a while," he laughed. Cindy shrugged her shoulders.

"Well, I was able to use some facial recognition software to isolate any photos that we had of Greg Hanes. There wasn't a whole lot but interestingly enough, he seemed to meet with the accountant fairly often. I figure Jay may have had Hanes picking up and delivering cash for him and that's what I think I was seeing in the photographs. But look at this one."

An image came up on the screen of two men sitting together at a bar. "It's Lulu's, do you know it?"

"Of course I know it, best macaroni and cheese in the city."

Cindy smiled as his face lit up at the mention of the restaurant. "Well, Mr. Gourmet, take another look at this photo. See how they're leaning in toward each other, looks like they're talking kind of quietly."

"Well wouldn't they, I mean it was illegal what they were doing."

"Sure, yeah, but look again." She sat back, looking at the image that filled her screen. It was a big dark wooden bar, backed by tall shelves filled with bottles of liquor and wine. In front the wooden counter was lined with place settings and a few glasses. Two empty plates made it look as if the men had finished their meal and were having a second drink together. "See how Hanes's hand is resting on the accountants arm? It's a casual movement but with their heads bent toward each other? They look like a couple to me, like they're interested in each other."

Cindy paged through four other shots taken from different meetings. Nothing appeared to be changing hands in any of them but once he knew to look for it, Ray could see the intimacy in the pairing. "But I thought Arnie was married." Cindy offered him a withering glance.

"And you never heard of a gay man getting married? Lowe was a good Catholic boy married to his high school sweetheart. I think the door on that closet was pretty firmly shut. Hanes didn't advertise his sexual preferences. He was a cop after all, but I think that door was at least ajar. Frankly, I think they look pretty damned happy together. You've got to figure they had a lot in common. From what we know, neither one of them volunteered to start working for the Warrens. They're both Pittsburgh guys who ended up with gambling debts that they couldn't pay."

"Gambling, that's how Jay got his hooks into Hanes? I wondered."

Cindy nodded. "I talked to his ex-partner for quite a while. He had a lot of good things to say about him, by the way, told me he was really smart and great at his job."

"So what happened?"

"The partner says that about six months before he resigned, Greg Hanes was given an undercover assignment to look into numbers running in the city. We think Walt's brother, James, is running it now but, at that time, it was run by Jay Warren. Hanes knew Warren from high school apparently and when the undercover role got out of his control and he got in over his head with gambling debts, Jay offered to help him out. Hanes's ex-partner seemed to think he resigned to keep the gambling debt a secret."

"So how did the partner know?"

"Beats me." Cindy shrugged. "You know how cop partners get, though, the good pairs really know one another. Plus, the guy's pissed; says his latest partner's so green he has to check his diapers."

"Did he know he was gay?"

73

"Yeah, said it didn't bother him any, although he knew Greg took some razzing about it at the precinct house."

Cindy turned back to her computer and pulled up two more photos, a little darker and hazier than the earlier ones. "These are from Lowe's funeral. See that figure at the back of the church? From what our agents on site said, he never got any closer to the coffin, or the widow, just stood there while people talked and then walked away."

"He looks pretty sad."

"Yep, I'd say it hit him pretty hard."

Ray stood and stretched out his back as Cindy continued to look at the photographs. "Okay, let's start looking into Arnie Lowe, see if we can get any more information about Hanes."

Cindy looked up the length of him. "But discreetly, right? We're not going to out some poor dead guy, are we?"

Ray sat back down abruptly. "Good point. Listen, why don't I go try to talk to some of Hanes' business clients while you talk with Lowe's wife. You've probably got more tact in your little finger than I've got in my whole body." Cindy laughed.

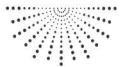

*a*n ear-piercing screech sounded in the pine trees not far from Greg's tent. He bolted upright, and tried hard not to scream in echo. It wasn't just the bird that had panicked him. It was the dream. He untangled himself from the hot sleeping bag and climbed backward out of the tent. For a moment he wished he still smoked.

He would have welcomed the companionable smell of tobacco tonight and found it surprising how strong that craving could be after so many years. The warm air seemed thick and humid for so late in the summer. He could feel the weight of it as he sat on top of the picnic table, his feet resting on the bench, waiting for the last skitters to ease away. The owl screeched again, now in the distance, its sound joining that of the frogs and insects that he'd grown more used to. He folded his arms on his knees and buried his face in them knowing that tears were not all that far below the surface. Fucking dream. Looking up suddenly, he slammed his fists on the table. How many nights had he been awakened like that, his heart racing, sweat forming along his hairline?

It was uncanny how the dream always began with the same sense of hope that he'd had that night. It was one of his high school's big football games and Greg had gone to watch with friends. One of them had a brother on the team and his friend, Lane, was the team's mascot. Together they were a loud group, raising a ruckus whenever one of the teams scored. Lane had to wear a ridiculous looking badger suit that he swore smelled like the worst tennis shoes ever. He'd let Greg try the head on just before the game and Greg thought the smell was even worse than he'd described.

It had finally become easier for Greg to admit to himself how much he liked Lane. They'd shared two classes and been put into enough groups together that they'd grown to like and respect each other. Class projects were always plagued with yahoos but they knew that they could count on each other to get the work done. They had also discovered a shared interest in old comic books and together they'd begun searching used bookshops around the city. That morning, they'd been standing in the cold waiting for one to open when Lane rested his hand on Greg's shoulder and looked at him pointedly. Greg was hesitant to look at him, afraid all of his teenage yearning would be visible enough to make Lane turn and run. But when he did look up finally, he saw on Lane's face a reflection of what he had been feeling. They both smiled, a little bit embarrassed, and made a plan to get together at Lane's house after the game. Sitting in the bleachers that night, Greg had hardly been able to stand the wait.

The game was a serious tromping by the other team and the two leaders of the team, Jay Warren and Jeff Stone, were clearly shocked at the booing and derision raining down on them from the stands. So many years later, it was becoming more and more difficult for Greg to separate the reality of the night from the dream it had become, but those two faces remained clear. As he had rounded the bleachers to head toward his car he heard a yell of pain.

There by the back door of the gym, Jay and Jeff were pounding the shit out of a frail boy wearing the uniform of the other team's mascot. Other sounds were muffled and blurred but Jay spitting out the words 'goddamned faggot' was clear enough to hear. Greg panicked and fled home without talking to Lane. He'd finally found the nerve to call and talk with him the next day but he could hear the distance in Lane's voice. Their friendship faded quickly. When Lane's family moved away that Christmas, Greg had been ashamed of the relief he'd felt.

The dream though, could shift everything around. Often Lane was the one being attacked and Greg was hiding under the bleachers, helpless, useless. Even worse, some nights he was the one administering the beating, shouting the hateful words. He rubbed his temples, remembering that in tonight's version the mascot in the suit had been Arnie. Tears came to Greg's eyes as he pictured the scene at Arnie's funeral. Dammit, he'd been too much of a coward to say anything then too. Fucking Jay Warren had taken everything he'd ever cared about.

Unable to sit any longer, Greg groped in the darkness of his tent until he found his sandals. There was a partial moon out and its light was enough for him to find the path through the dunes toward the water. He walked carefully, trying not to disturb the other campers although a snorer in one of the distant tents seemed to be covering up any noise that he was making.

Shucking his sandals at the edge of the dune, Greg walked out onto the damp sand where the cool water shifted over and back across the tops of his feet. He began to walk, the rhythm of the water calming his jangled nerves. Here the air felt less humid and he was able to breathe deeply and think more clearly than he could back at the campsite. Lane and Arnie, he mused. There had been others in between, a few relationships that he thought might have become more serious but those other faces had become even more difficult to remember. As a beat cop, Greg had needed to prove himself again and again, sometimes recklessly, before he began to be respected as a cop, rather than an oddity. Once he'd made detective, the pressure had eased somewhat and he had enjoyed working with his partner, a solid family man who'd never seemed to have any issues with Greg's sexuality. They'd been an effective pair until Jay Warren had fucked up his life again. Greg stopped, poked his foot at a dark shell and watched a small crab dash into the water. He could feel the disapproving eyes of his gambler's anonymous sponsor. He was responsible for his gambling problem, not Jay Warren. He paused, owned it again in his head and resumed walking.

Like every train of thought that wound its way through his head these days, it derailed back in the present. What was he doing on this island? What did he think he could accomplish? He was hiding for sure, but how could you tell the difference between prudence and cowardice? His friend Marybeth had faced off with Jay in the restaurant and had the nerve to steal his gun and shoot him. What had Greg ever done? He hadn't helped Arnie, that was for damned sure. Had he been a fool to leave the restaurant the way he did? Should he have stayed, named Tony Morelli as the guy who'd delivered the beating, taken his chances with the good guys maybe? But what was to stop the FBI from arresting him along with everyone else in the Warren ring? He'd done surveillance, delivered cash, of course, the FBI would arrest him, they wouldn't have any other choice. So here he was on some speck of land smaller than a single borough of the city, nearly broke, homeless, a gambler, a coward, walking and waiting for dawn.

CHAPTER TWELVE

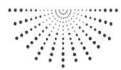

*T*he next week, Carolyn was pleased to see a few of the plates that she was juggling settle. The permit for the pre-school had come from the state. As a certified teacher with steady funding, the paperwork had come through fairly easily. Of course she hadn't mentioned the possible end to her funding yet, but it was a weight at the back of her mind through everything she did. The license she was pursuing for the special needs portion of the center that would allow her to diagnose and program for special needs children, was taking a little more time. Pairing with the local public school system and having Dr. Susan Gilbert on staff had helped but the state was looking for a larger roster of staff before they would allow her to move forward. That morning, she was on the phone with her friend Janine in Baltimore. "It's so good to talk to you. How's April? How's Baltimore?" Carolyn leaned back, picturing her friend in her cramped art studio, working away on one of her over-sized canvases.

"It's good, but we miss you so much! April keeps looking for PJ to come play with her. Aren't you tired of that millionaire's life yet?"

Carolyn laughed remembering the court challenge that might cause her return. "Well, not quite yet, I guess!"

She could hear the hesitation in her friend's voice. "Did Alex call you? Was it okay that I told him where you were?"

"Yes, well he showed up here. I was pretty surprised, but PJ was thrilled."

"So what's going on?"

"He came to interview for a job near here, as a firefighting instructor. He says he wants to get back into our lives but I really don't know what to think."

"What about that other firefighter? I forget her name."

"Apparently there was a really big fire and his friend Juan was killed. Chris was injured really badly and afterwards, fell for her physical therapist."

"Wow, that's a lot to take in. So she's out of the picture and you're a wealthy woman and he decides it's time to come back?"

Carolyn stood and walked around to lean on the front of her desk. "I didn't tell him about the money."

"What does he think you're doing in that mansion then? You said he came over, right?"

"Uh, I kind of made it sound like it was just a job. It would complicate everything so much more if he found out. I'm already as confused as I can be. Right now he's back in Baltimore getting everything together to move. I guess I'll see what happens once he settles in."

"Are you still interested?"

"Wow, that's an even harder question, one I don't think I can answer right now. But listen, I wanted to ask you something else. How determined are you to stay in Baltimore this winter?"

"What do you mean? Things are a little tight, but April and I are managing."

Carolyn detected a tone of hurt in her friend's voice. "Oh, no, no, no, that's not what I meant. Listen, you know I'm trying to start a pre-school here and the truth is, I could use another certified teacher to help me. You're still qualified to teach art here in Pennsylvania, right? I can't afford to pay a whole lot right now but I could provide you and April with a living area as well as space for you to paint. The classroom will be a half-day program so you'd have plenty of time to work. Plus, I would love having you and April here in the house with PJ and me."

"Wow, Carolyn. Are you sure about all of that? I would love to do some teaching again but I don't know about uprooting April."

"Is Sean still staying there?" She heard her friend hesitate.

"Ah, yeah, to be honest Carolyn, he and his new girlfriend are living here now. I hope you're not hurt by that."

Carolyn took a deep breath and pictured Sean with someone new, but she had to admit, it really didn't send any flutterings one way or another. "You know, Janine, it's okay. Does she deserve him at least?"

Janine laughed. "Well, she's pretty good at calling him on his bullshit so I do tend to like her. And April is crazy about her. I always like to trust a child's judgment."

"So what do you think? Could they take care of your house for a while if you came here?"

"I'm just not sure. Can I think about it? How long of a commitment are you looking for?"

"I would love for you to stay forever of course, but realistically, I'm just thinking from now till the end of the year at this point." She smiled. "We could celebrate Christmas together and then you could decide."

"Till Christmas, huh?"

Carolyn could picture her friend sitting in her studio, April playing in the corner with her own little paint set. She crossed her fingers as she waited on the line. Finally her friend came back on.

"All right, truth here, I would like to get out of Baltimore for a while. Between you and me, Patsy is in pretty rough shape right now and it would be nice to put a little distance between us, you know?"

Carolyn didn't know Janine's ex-girlfriend very well, having met her only once. Patsy had moved back home to New Jersey and gone into re-hab for several months, not long after April was born. She and Janine had planned on getting married and raising April together, but the relationship had not survived the new baby, or Patsy's drug and alcohol habit. Carolyn was sad to hear she was still struggling. "I'm so sorry, Janine. I thought she was doing better."

"Yeah, she was and then she wasn't. Listen, let me talk to Sean and think about all of this for a little while."

Carolyn was so pleased that she was at least considering it. "Thank you so much for even thinking about it, Janine. If this doesn't work out, I hope you'll plan to come for the holidays, anyway!"

Janine laughed. "Carolyn, I would give anything to see that big mansion of yours decorated for the holidays so that's a definite yes! I'll talk to you soon."

Carolyn was happy that Janine hadn't rejected the idea outright. They'd been best friends for such a long time, it was the one ache of leaving Baltimore behind. She was crossing her fingers now, hoping for the best. The house phone on her desk rang once and she picked it up.

"Miss, Dr. Wright is here to see you." Rupert announced.

She still had not convinced him to call her Carolyn, Miss was the most relaxed he seemed to get. "Thank you Rupert, would you send him to the library for me?"

It was only a few minutes later when Charlie appeared at the door, unwinding his long woolen scarf and handing it and his hat to the butler. Rupert nodded before stepping away. Carolyn moved to the door and gave Charlie a big hug before ushering him to the comfortable seats by the fireplace. He rubbed his hands together and leaned toward the warmth. He sat back then, pulling his sweater down into place. "It's kind of a damp, cold morning out there, you can tell winter is really on its way. How are you?"

Carolyn was happy to settle into the deep, cushioned chair as well. "Rupert asked me this morning if I'd like to have a fire today. I couldn't resist. How are you? Too nasty out for your morning walk today?"

He shook his head. "No, I pushed on through, got my two miles in." He twisted his wrist to show her the fitness tracker he was now sporting. "A friend in my wine club gave me this. We've been meeting up to walk for a few weeks now." He shrugged. "It sure is better getting out with a friend."

Carolyn could see the sadness pull at his shoulders and she thought again of the uncle she had found only to lose before getting to know him. Charlie and Edward had been friends for more than 50 years. She knew that he was missing him. She worried that coming to the house and working with her on the school would make it even harder for him, but he had insisted that being busy was the best antidote to grief. "I'm glad you found someone to walk with, Charlie."

Just then there was a soft knock on the door and Helen came in bearing a tray with a carafe, two, thick, painted coffee mugs and a small plate of banana bread. Charlie beamed at her. "You spoil us, Helen!"

Carolyn took one of the mugs and inhaled deeply.

"So, Charlie," Carolyn leaned back into her seat. "What have you found out? I'm terrified someone's going to throw us out of here and expect me to pay all of the money back."

Charlie took a sip of the coffee and broke off a section of the bread. He took his time before responding. Carolyn grew even more alarmed. He chewed carefully and then finally answered. "I won't sugarcoat it. Jay Warren has enlisted his uncle James's help and the man has some very powerful attorneys. They're pushing hard."

"What exactly is the challenge? Do PJ and I need to do DNA testing or something? Is that the line they're taking?"

He nodded. "It's one of the lines and frankly, I think it's in your best interest to cooperate. There's a police station not far from here where you could have it done." He pulled a plastic packet out of his pocket and set it down between them. "I think we should do our own test as well, though, just to be sure." He paused before continuing. "Are any of Edward's things here, anything we could submit as a DNA sample from him?" Carolyn watched his face as the grief moved across it.

"I wasn't sure what to do with all of his things so I just closed off that bedroom and left everything as it was. I'll get whatever samples I can find and send them along with ours. But, I have to ask, do you have doubts, Charlie? It's not like Marybeth figured out I was her daughter through any sort of scientific means. What if it turns out that I'm a fraud of some sort?"

His face changed then and the sadness was replaced by determination. "Now, none of that. I knew Marybeth when she was Sarah at Penn State and you remain the spitting image of her. Edward admitted that he had a hand in things when you were first put up for adoption so he was even more certain. I just think we would find DNA results reassuring. All you have to do is take a swab of yours and PJ's cheeks and mail it off. It's not hard." He held the mug in his hand, letting its warmth seep in. "It's not their main tactic, though, I have to tell you. They're challenging Edward's mental capacity and they're blaming Marybeth. They're painting her in a really bad light, saying she started this whole search for you in order to steal his money."

Carolyn had first met her birth mother, Marybeth Rogers, that summer in Baltimore. She had been in the witness protection program until Jay Warren was killed in a plane crash and she came searching for Carolyn, the infant she'd had to give up so many years before. It had been strange at first, meeting this woman after so many years, but Carolyn liked her immediately and was thrilled by the connection. She believed Marybeth when she said she'd been shocked to meet Jay's Uncle Edward and learn of the money he wanted to pass on to Carolyn and PJ.

Carolyn shot to her feet and paced a short track in front of their chairs. "But that is so crazy! She was just looking for me! She didn't know about Edward, or his money. I'll never believe that!"

Charlie waited, took a long sip of his coffee and when she'd collapsed back into her chair, he continued. "Now, now, you know I am squarely on your side. In fact, I was with Edward through his search and I know for a fact that he instigated it, not her. I can testify to all of that if it comes down to a trial, but right now, I think they're focused on trying to scare us." He spread his hands wide in front of him. "After all, scaring people is what that organization has been doing for decades. It's why Marybeth was in hiding. And keep in mind, just because Jay's in jail doesn't mean he isn't wielding influence. Now, don't get me wrong, we have good, powerful lawyers too. They just wanted me to let you know what's going on. We're going to win, I feel it." He looked around the library. "We'll win because Eddie would want us to win." He stood and brushed the crumbs off his knee onto a small napkin. "Come, show me this classroom you've been working on."

Carolyn and Charlie carried their mugs with them and walked together to see the classroom. Carolyn was so proud of her work it was all she could do not to ramble on and on. When she'd received the email to stop spending, she'd let the contractors finish what they were doing and then she had continued working on her own to paint and decorate the large atrium that she was converting into a pre-school classroom. Different sections of the room now sported a variety of colors so that the overall affect was a wide rainbow whose rays came together over the broad, windowed doorway to the outside. She was pleased at how it had turned out, especially when she heard Charlie catch his breath. "Carolyn, I love it!"

"Oh, I'm so glad. Each section of color is going to be an activity area. She drew him toward the deep blue wall where she had begun arranging a classroom space with the smallest chairs she could find and a dozen, small fat pillows, just right for little bottoms. "This is where we'll start and end each morning so that they get some practice in regular school expectations." They moved around the color wheel until they were in front of a broad yellow wall. "This will be the art area. I have a lead on an art teacher who might be willing to join us."

They continued to walk around the perimeter, discussing the plans she had for the different sections. She hated having to tell him about the one-way mirror but he didn't seem overly concerned. "That's a luxury, really, we won't need it to get started." They worked their way back to the library where they settled back in their chairs, refilled their cups from the carafe Helen had left and split the last piece of banana bread.

"Are you still thinking about just a half-day program?"

Carolyn nodded, "I am. Down the road I'd like to see it go to a full day. I have the pre-school permit from the state now and I'm working with the neighborhood elementary to supply us with a part-time social worker and speech pathologist to help with the evaluations." She moved her arm in a broad sweep. "Rather than buy things, I began searching around the house for furniture that we could re-purpose and I found a good table and chairs for the conference room as well as a smaller table and chairs for the testing area. I've started to reach out to the community for a few classroom volunteers and so far I have five children lined up as well as one special needs referral."

Charlie was impressed with everything, both the physical work of remodeling the space and the more mundane business side of things. "Do you have a start date in mind?"

"Within a month for sure. But Charlie, you have to tell me, is it foolish to go ahead when there's so much uncertainty in front of us?" She leaned forward anxiously.

Charlie set his cup down and stood, reaching for the hat and scarf that had been left folded by the door. "I specifically asked our lawyers and they think we should go ahead with our plans. You're going to be bringing in some income in fees once you're up and running so they think that only helps our case." He spun his hat in his hand and smiled at her. "I'm impressed, here Carolyn, really impressed. And I'm glad you're letting me be a part of it all."

She laughed. "Well, Charlie, I did drop your name on my paperwork with the state, you know. When you've got Dr. Charles Wright, professor emeritus from the Penn State School of Education on your governing board, it can only speed things up!" She rose and gave him another big hug. "I'll send you an email when I know about my friend. And, don't forget, I'm planning to have an *Open House* to get everything off to a good start!"

He smiled and gestured toward his wrist. "My walking friend is a retired party planner. I'll have her give you a call. She's had to listen to all of my endless talk about this place. She's eager to help." He waved his hat, "we're on our way, girl!" before plopping it on his baldhead and moving toward the door.

Carolyn waited until she knew he was gone before taking a moment for a quick little happy dance behind her desk. Throwing caution to the wind, she took a moment to go online and re-order the mirrored window. The heck with it, she thought, and put it on her own credit card just to be safe. She considered buckling down to do more work, but decided instead to find PJ and Rusty and just play! On her way down the hall though, she had to laugh. So, his walking friend is a woman, and a party planner. What could be better?

CHAPTER THIRTEEN

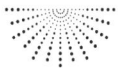

*P*amela Lowe was not what Cindy had expected. A tall, striking blonde in a power suit that probably cost more than a month's pay was waiting impatiently at the door when Cindy arrived. "Good afternoon. I'm Agent Cindy O'Brien with the FBI. Are you Pamela Lowe? Could I talk with you for a little bit?"

"Yes, I'm Pamela. Do you have new information on my husband's death? Have you found out who hit him?" The woman was cordial enough, ushering the agent into the house, but it was clear she hadn't much time for the procedure.

"Uh, may I sit?"

"Certainly," Pamela directed her to a stylish but uncomfortable looking wooden chair while she settled on the end of the plush couch.

Cindy pulled herself up straight and opened a black leather portfolio. "I'm sorry, Pamela, we don't have any more information on who was driving the car that hit Mr. Lowe, but we do have some new information on why we think your husband was hit."

Pamela Lowe's bluster seemed to evaporate as she allowed herself to sink into the sofa. "So it was deliberate after all." Cindy waited out the long pause. "It was the Warrens, wasn't it?"

Cindy sat up even taller, shocked at the woman's tone. "I have to ask, did you know that your husband was working for the Warrens? There was no mention of that in the interview you gave to the police after the accident."

Pamela stood and opened the window beside the sofa before pulling a cigarette and small lighter from her purse on the table by the door. She lit it carefully and then stood with her hand near the open window. "I'm sorry, I know I should have spoken up, but frankly, I was afraid they might come after me or my children."

"We could have offered protection, Mrs. Lowe."

"With all due respect, Agent, when has police protection ever protected someone from the Warrens? I grew up over in York, in the center of the state, but even there the name Warren was known." She began to pace a few steps forward and back from the window. "You have to understand, I loved my husband dearly, but we weren't everything that people thought we were."

"Family secrets you mean?"

Pamela nodded. "You could say that." She spoke slowly, pausing often to look out the window as she took puffs of the nearly forgotten cigarette. "I can't remember a time when I didn't know Arnie. Our families were close before either of us were born and as we got older we were constantly brought together for one activity or another." She smiled with a warmth that Cindy hadn't seen before. "We were good friends, co-conspirators if you were, before we ever fell in love and got married. Of course our parents were thrilled when we made the announcement but I always thought that I was a little bit more excited about everything than Arnie. But you know how men are with weddings." She gestured with the slim cigarette. "I figured that was all there was to it."

Cindy waited for it. Had the wife known all along of his other sexual interests, of the trysts with Greg Hanes?

Pamela crushed out the remainder of the cigarette and sat on the arm of the sofa. "What I didn't know at the time was that he'd lost our honeymoon money on a couple of horse races at the track. Don't get me wrong, over the years we worked through it, he got the help he needed and I was successful enough in my work that we were able to weather any financial storms. Frankly, now that our girls are getting ready for middle school and high school, I thought Arnie had finally gotten past it. But, one night about two weeks before he was killed, Arnie and I were out on a date at this charity event being held downtown."

She stood and paced the center of the room between the sofa and the wide fireplace. "It was in one of those fancy hotels, I can't remember which one. We were sitting in the bar afterwards having a nightcap when Jay Warren came up from behind us and slapped Arnie on the back. It was supposed to look like a friendly gesture but," she shrugged, "I could tell it wasn't. Arnie stepped away from the bar with him and when he got back, he paid the tab and we left. After that he was silent, driving so carefully, checking in his rearview mirror the whole way home. I started to say something several times but he just shook his head at me. Once we got home, he took me into our bathroom, turned the shower on and the fan before he whispered the truth to me. Frankly, I felt like such a fool for not having noticed that he'd been struggling with the gambling again, that I really didn't know what to think. The one thing he did say though, over and over, was that he never brought any of their business, any of their information near the house, or our family."

"Did you have any idea where he did keep the information? There's an awful lot that an accountant would know about an operation like the Warrens."

"I don't know," she shrugged. "I was so relieved there was nothing here that I never asked. In fact, I'm pretty sure that while we were at the funeral for Arnie, someone came and went through the house. It wasn't wrecked or anything, but I could tell things were out of place."

"Did you report it?"

Pamela shook her head and sank back onto the sofa. "No, I was too afraid. I figured if they searched the house and didn't find anything then this was the safest place we could be. I just carried on like the hit-and-run was just that, a fluke. I let my girls think that, too." She looked up at Cindy, her concern rising again. "You're not going to question them, are you? I know for a fact that Arnie would never have put them in any kind of jeopardy. He was a good man, a good father, Agent O'Brien."

Cindy smiled. "I don't see any need to talk to your girls, ma'am. But do you have some ideas about where he *could* have kept the information? I'm pretty sure he was managing a fair amount of money and he would have had to keep records on it."

Pamela stood and gestured toward the kitchen. "Would you like some coffee? I'm sorry for having been so rude to start with. I've just been a bit of a wreck as you can imagine. Let's come out here. She pointed toward a comfortable looking leather chair and Cindy sat at a beautiful kitchen table as she prepared the coffee.

"This is a lovely home, Pamela."

"Oh thank you," she smiled. "We had it remodeled last year and I just love it." She set a bright red mug in front of Cindy and sat down again. "Arnie was a genius with computers, Agent O'Brien, and I know for a fact that his lap top would have been in the car with him. I asked the police and there was not one found at the scene. I'm sure he would have encrypted the information but probably not in a way that they couldn't have gotten through it."

"Would he have kept a back-up do you think?"

Pamela smiled again. "Knowing Arnie, I would have bet on it." She laughed. "Bad pun, I know." Then took a more serious tone. "One of Arnie's favorite words was 'leverage'. When we talked that night in the bathroom, he said he was working hard on figuring a way to get out from under them." She shrugged, "I'm just afraid he ran out of time before he could finish it."

"Did you ever see him with anyone else from the Warren organization?"

"Not that I knew of. We mostly had friends in common, and we didn't go out often once we had the girls. He did mention a friend from work named Greg and I know they got a drink together once in a while, but I don't remember anyone else. I recognized Jay Warren from the newspaper."

"Did Arnie have any particular hang outs or places that he liked to go? " Cindy took a sip of the coffee, afraid once more of saying too much.

"No, not really, at least not here in the city."

"Was there somewhere else that he liked to go?"

"Well, it's kind of corny, but he did like to visit this little state park on the coast of North Carolina where he worked as a teenager. We used to take family vacations there when the girls were little, but we haven't been there in quite some time so I can't imagine that would be of any help."

Cindy finished her coffee and closed the portfolio before standing up and offering her hand. "Thank you so much, Pamela. I can't imagine how painful this must be for you and I really do appreciate your taking the time to talk with me. I'm so sorry for your loss."

Pamela nodded and walked with her toward the front door. "Thank you, I appreciate your discretion in all of this." Cindy nodded and walked toward her car, never noticing the man in dark glasses sitting in the small sedan down the street.

She returned to the office after the main shift of agents had left but was happy to see that Ray was still hunched over the computer at his desk. "Hey, what're you doing here so late?"

Ray looked up and smiled broadly before answering in a low voice. "Waiting for you, of course."

She smiled back and answered with what she hoped was a coy tone, "Of course?"

He leaned back in his chair with his feet on the lower desk drawer that was slightly open. "I don't mean to get ahead of myself," he looked up uncertainly, "but I was hoping maybe we could get a bite to eat." He paused awkwardly, watching her face for a sign.

She plopped down into his visitor's chair and gave up on trying the coy approach. She was just too happy to be seeing him to get into all of the stupid games that people seemed to expect. She put her feet up on the outer edge of the drawer and leaned in. "I would love to get a bite and no, you're not getting ahead of yourself."

He smiled and replaced the glasses that had been resting on the top of his head. "Was it a good interview?"

"Yeah, really good. Would it be okay if we picked up some takeout and then went over to my place? I'd like to talk about it but not where we could be heard."

He finished powering down his computer and grabbed his Steelers jacket off the back of his chair. "Sure thing, what do you want to get?"

She stood. "How about some mac and cheese from Lulu's? I figure we can give the place a quick look around while we're there."

"Lulu's it is!" He grinned at her as they got onto the elevator.

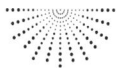

CHAPTER FOURTEEN

*P*ete was not surprised to learn that James Warren had already taken over Walt's place and seemed to be making himself quite at home. Pete had been met at the door by a beautiful young woman who'd ushered him up to Walt's old office before disappearing silently back down the stairs. James was sitting behind the desk that Walt had so cherished. It was an antique from his wife's family and he'd kept it meticulously clean. But now it was piled with papers and food wrappers and the room smelled vaguely of body odor and spaghetti. James was even larger than Pete remembered and he had to work hard not to imagine Jabba the Hutt with James's features. He waited politely for James to begin.

"So," the big man snorted, "I thought you were supposed to be dead, Turner, how is it you're standing here? Wait, don't tell me, another Jay Warren fuck up, am I right?"

Pete remained standing, lowering his head briefly before raising it up to face the man squarely and answering. "Jay's fucked himself up for sure, but I'm here because I'm smarter than he was. It looks like you're running things now and I'm ready to step up, do my part."

"Your part, what the fuck does that mean? I got people already, what the hell am I supposed to do with you?"

"Well," Pete remained standing but drew himself up straight. "I assume," he gestured to the room around him, "you've put your hands on all of Walt's records or you wouldn't be sitting where you are."

"That's right," he gestured at the cluttered desktop. "Got everything running just fine."

"What about Jay's records, you got them too?"

James huffed as he reached for the large soda cup sitting atop a pile of papers. "What records? Walt's books look pretty comprehensive to me. Money's rolling in just fine."

Pete paused, uncertain whether to spill what he knew about the extent of Jay's other business dealings or keep it to himself. Clearly, James thought he had it all going on already. Maybe it was best if he kept on thinking that, while Pete did a little investigating of his own. He decided to take a more deferential tone.

"Okay then, what about work? You got any for me, or for Jay's boys, Tony and Vince? They're still waiting at the damn safe house for directions."

James nodded, sipping loudly from the cup. "I can always use some muscle like those guys. I'll give 'em a call, see if they're up to my standards, I suppose. But what about you, what kind of work you lookin' for? You're getting kind of long in the tooth, aren't you? Maybe you should've just stayed down there in the tropics, retired like."

One of three cell phones sitting on the desk buzzed insistently. James picked it up, the device looking like a doll's toy in his thick paw. "What?" He waited, then jabbed his finger into the desk. "Then get the fuck over there, for God's sake. Why do you think we left the damn bug there in the first place? Jesus," he slapped the phone back onto the desk. "Fuckin' morons. Device picks up an FBI agent at the old accountant's place and they got to call me to figure out what to do?"

"I could go check it out for you." Pete reached in his pocket and pulled out his keys.

James gave him a steady look before nodding at him. "Okay, I'll call my guy off. You let me know what you find out. Maybe you can be useful after all." He shifted his chair away from Pete and picked up the phone again.

Pete expected to see the stunning young woman again but no one appeared. In fact, the house sounded empty as he hurried back down the stairs and out to his car.

Pete'd known the accountant, Arnie Lowe, for a while, had kind of liked the guy he supposed, but Jay had ordered him to take him out so he'd taken him out. Staging a hit-and-run wasn't rocket science after all. But now, after all this time, what would an FBI agent be doing back at the widow's house? He made the drive quickly, the height of the evening's rush hour traffic still about an hour away. He pulled over to the curb two doors down and spotted a newish Jeep parked on the street in front of the house. He walked by it casually, spotted a dark blazer tossed on the seat and figured it to be the agent's car. He walked on a ways but the neighborhood seemed quiet so he turned around, patting his jacket pockets and pretending to have forgotten something. When he passed the Jeep again, he took a quick second to attach a tracking beacon under the left fender. He got back into his car to wait but had only been there for a minute or two before a woman with curly dark hair said her good-byes at the door and walked to her car. While he debated whether to follow her or approach the house, his phone rang. He pulled it out of the cup holder, recognizing James's voice immediately. "See anything?"

"Agent's leaving now. Want me to follow her?"

"Her, Jesus, fucking women in the fucking FBI. No, don't follow her. You know where my old house is, right? It's over on the west side of the city. I've got the surveillance center set up over there now. Go see my guys, find out what was said and take care of it, all of it. You got that?"

"You got it, chief." He hung up and dropped the phone back down before turning over the engine. "Chief, what the hell was that?" He kicked himself over that the whole drive over.

Pete pulled in to park in the alley behind the house, just as a second car pulled in beside him. The old blue Camaro was practically touching the ground as the two huge men emerged. "What the hell are you two bozos doing here?"

Tony spoke up first. "We got a call, said to come on over here and help out. We're so sick of that shithole safe house, we hurried on over. What are you doing here?"

"Following up on some surveillance. Listen, here's some free advice. You two keep what you know about Jay's operations to yourselves, you hear me? Don't volunteer anything." He locked his car with the remote and leaned in toward the two brothers. "I'm thinking about getting something going on my own, you hear me? Might be something in it for you two boys down the road if you don't fuck it up first."

"Fuck what up? Vince asked.

"Say nothing, are we clear, nothing?"

The two big men looked at each other and shrugged. "You got it Pete. We'd rather work for you than that fat slug any day. Just let us know."

They exchanged a quick nod before the two big men headed in the back door. Pete took the time to walk around the front of the house and ring the doorbell. He hoped it would piss off the men working inside just a little bit. He guessed he'd figured right when an old guy in a hideous brown sweater yanked the door open and glared at him. "You the surveillance guy I'm supposed to see?"

"What the hell are you doing at the front door? This is a nice neighborhood, don't you know anything?"

Pete grinned to himself but kept his face neutral as he followed him in the door. "Sorry about that. I've been away for a while."

"Come in, asshole, boss wants you to hear something."

"You got it." He followed the older man in to a dining room that had been converted into a sort of office. The room was ringed with computers, two of which were occupied by teenage boys with headsets. Pete looked at the older man who'd led him in. "What the fuck is this? He's got babies working for him over here now?" Pete gestured at the two young men.

The old guy was easily a foot taller than Pete and powerful enough to shove him against the wall as he pulled out his pistol. "Those are my grandsons, you asshole, and they already know more about computers than you ever will so just shut the fuck up before I fuck you up." He raised the gun to Pete's eye level as he lifted his hands in surrender.

"My mistake." Pete lowered his arms and put his hands in his pockets, hiding their slight shake. He waited as the man rapped the nearest listener on the shoulder to get his attention. The young man lowered his headphones and looked up.

"Boss wants him to hear what you've got from the accountant's house."

"Hi, I'm Pete," he offered his hand to the young man.

The man from the door shoved a hand at his chest. "He don't need to know your name. Just sit your ass in the chair and listen." As Pete dropped into the chair he caught a glimpse of Tony and Vince coming in from the kitchen. "What the fuck now?" the man muttered as he left the room to meet what looked like the new muscle.

Pete didn't make eye contact with them but turned instead to the young man. He was dressed casually in torn jeans and an old red T-shirt that had lost whatever decoration it once had. He was the young version of skinny with traces of acne still visible across his forehead. Frizzy hair was flattened on the sides where fat headphones were perched.

"Okay, let's hear what you've got." Pete listened once, then had the young man run it again. Then he took off the headphones. "So what do you think?'"

The young man shrugged. "They don't pay me to think around here." He turned back to the equipment but Pete tapped him on the shoulder.

"I want to know what you think." He waited. The young man looked him up and down, then over his shoulder at the closed door to the listening room before shrugging his shoulders and setting down his headphones.

"I think the widow doesn't know dick, that's what I think. And, I think the agent knows more than she's saying."

"How can you tell?"

"It's not my first day on the job, you know?"

"What makes you think the widow doesn't know anything?"

"Well, she sure didn't know her husband was swinging for both teams, did she? I think the agent might of known, though."

Pete was taken aback. He'd never picked up that vibe in his dealings with the accountant. "How can you tell?" The young man shrugged again but Pete sensed a real pride in his skills.

"I don't know, you do this much listening, you start to hear the pauses as well as the talking. I think the agent was holding back."

"What did you mean about the husband? You think he was gay?"

"Don't they call it 'bi' if you go both ways?" The young man shrugged again, feigning an indifference that Pete could tell was practiced rather than genuine. "I heard him on the phone last winter making a date with some guy he called Greg."

Pete leaned forward resting his forearms on his legs. "You remember that far back?"

The young man looked at Pete with an expression that held a multitude of meanings. "I remember everything, dude."

Pete smiled at him and stood, resting his hand on his shoulder as he leaned in and whispered. "They're not paying you enough and you know a lot more than you let on. Keep it that way and I may be able to offer you a whole hell of a lot more down the road."

He looked the older man up and down as he put his headphones back into place. "Promises, promises," he muttered and returned to his work.

Pete debated whether to report back to James or not, but decided it was better to stay in the man's good graces for now. Once he was back in his car he sent a quick text to a buddy to get the address that went with the license plate, then a second one to James. *WIDOW DIDN'T KNOW SHIT. AGENT GOT NOTHING. WILL FOLLOW UP.* Then he took his time driving, trying to sort out his next steps.

If the accountant knew Hanes that well, there might have been more going on than Jay ever knew and certainly more than James would understand. Time to pay a visit to that busybody of an agent.

CHAPTER FIFTEEN

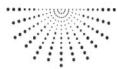

*R*ay and Cindy took their time walking the few blocks east to Lulu's. Once they were away from the station, they even dared to hold hands. But fall was working hard at turning into winter and they were happy once they found themselves inside the warm, noisy restaurant. While Ray ordered their food, Cindy walked over to the long black bar that ran the length of one of the restaurant's walls. The bartender, an older man with a solid paunch and laugh lines around his eyes, came over as soon as he was free. Cindy showed him her badge. "Hi, I'm Agent Cindy O'Brien with the FBI. Can I ask you a few questions?"

"Sure," he glanced at the badge and then reached for a nearby glass. He held it out toward her. "Can I get you something to drink?"

"No, thank you. I'm fine. My," she paused for a moment, unsure what he was exactly, "uh, my friend is ordering us some take out." She pulled up the photograph of Hanes and the accountant on her phone and turned it to face him. "Do you recognize these two men? We think this photo was taken here sometime last winter. Have you been working here that long?"

The man laughed a deep rumble and Cindy could see exactly

where the laugh lines had come from. "Honey, my mama was Lulu and I've been here my whole life." He took the phone and enlarged the picture slightly before nodding to her. "Sure, I recognize them. They liked eating here at my bar, picked it even when there were plenty of tables open."

"What else do you remember about them?"

He cleared away a dirty place setting and then picked up a white cloth and began wiping down an area. "I don't know, they were nice guys, good tippers," he chuckled. "I tend to remember the good tippers. They seemed like pretty good friends to me." He paused. "Maybe more than friends?" His eyebrows lifted. "If you know what I mean?" He stood tall, the rag resting in his hand.

"What made you think that?"

He shrugged, "Not sure really. Little things I guess, sometimes they'd split a beer or steal fries back and forth. They seemed closer than most guys would sitting here. Didn't bother me none, love is love as far as I'm concerned and if you're lucky enough to find it, never figured it was my place to complain. They looked happy sitting here eating, that's all. Wait, the one guy," he turned back to the photograph and pointed at Arnie. "He died, didn't he? I seem to remember hearing about that this spring. Drunk driver, wasn't it?"

Cindy took the phone back and tucked it into her pocket. "Well, hit-and-run."

"Bastards," he slammed the rag onto the counter. "What kind of filthy low life does that? I swear." He paused, then drew a tray of silverware toward him and the top napkin off of a tall pile. He began rolling silverware sets for the tables, a task he seemed to do by feel, working rapidly without really looking down. "I guess that's why I haven't seen them in here in so long." He paused, "Come to think of it, I did see the other guy in here one time, early in the summer maybe?" He paused in his task. "He looked so sad as I recall. He picked up some take-out, still left me a tip even though I didn't do anything. Is he in some kind of trouble, Miss, I mean Agent?"

"No, we'd just like to talk with him about his friend. Can I ask, did you ever see them doing any sort of business deals?"

He looked up, a roll of silverware in each hand. "Business?" he seemed puzzled. "Not really, I mean there was this bag that they kept trading back and forth, it just looked like some kind of inside joke between the two of them."

"Did you ever see what was in it?"

He placed the setting on top of the growing pile. "Nah, like I said, it seemed like a joke, an excuse to get together like."

Ray walked over then, a large take-out bag in his hand. Cindy nodded at the bar tender and handed him her card. "Thank you so much for talking with me, uh..."

He reached a wide hand over the bar, Chester Briggs, ma'am but folks just call me CB."

"Good to meet you, CB. If you think of anything else, give me a call."

He saluted her with the card in his hand. "Will do. Hope you find the bastards that hit that guy."

Cindy waved and she and Ray headed out. It wasn't far to her apartment but she realized part way there that it would be the first time he'd ever seen it. Shit, had she left it clean? She couldn't quite remember. She started to apologize as she unlocked the door, then stopped in mid-stride once she had the door open. She held her hand against Ray's chest. "Stop, something's not right." She could see into the small living room where her desk was on its side and photographs from the wall had been shattered against the coffee table.

Ray looked over her head and set the take-out bag down as they both drew their weapons. He gestured her right as he went left. It didn't take long to clear the few rooms. The living room and the desk had taken the worst of it. The bedroom had been tossed but not with the same type of malice used in the living room. They met in the center of the room and Cindy made the call to the local police station. When she got off the phone he gestured to her to follow him into the hall where he picked up the bag of food. "What do you think happened?" he asked in a low voice.

Cindy turned her back to the ruined apartment and stood on tiptoes to whisper in his ear. "It doesn't feel like a random break in. I think someone is listening in at the widow's house and," she gestured toward the room, "maybe here as well. Let's meet the police downstairs, not here."

Ray nodded and reached his arm around her as they walked back down the stairs.

They were both starving by the time the officers finished with the scene and left. In tacit agreement, Cindy and Ray had kept their suspicions to themselves, then gone from room to room looking for listening devices. The one in the bedroom was easy enough to find, hidden under the nightstand. There didn't seem to be one in the bathroom but there was another in the kitchen and two in the living room. Cindy picked them up carefully and set them all on the bed before closing the door. She put the food in to warm and got them each a beer from the refrigerator before sitting down across from Ray at her small kitchen table. They continued to talk in low voices.

"What do you think we should do?" Ray asked.

Cindy took a sip of beer as she thought. "I want to flush them all down the toilet but I think that would just arouse suspicion and I have no idea how they would retaliate. Think we could leave a couple and destroy the rest?

"Probably," Ray retrieved the food from the microwave and tipped a serving onto each plate. "When I set some up I usually figure a few will malfunction. Which ones do you think we should leave?"

Cindy took a bite of the food, glad that they had something as comforting as mac and cheese. "I guess I should leave one in the living room and maybe one here in the kitchen? Think that's enough? I sure as hell don't want them listening in my bedroom." She blushed as she heard Ray laughing.

"Definitely not the bedroom." He smiled and reached his hand out for her. "I think this means we're on the right track, don't you? If we disturbed things enough to make them strike out like this, then maybe they've got something to hide. We'll have to be more careful, though."

Cindy nodded. "I didn't even think of bugs at Arnie's house and that was after she told me someone had gone through the place during the funeral." Ray looked up surprised.

"You never got around to telling me about the interview. She suspected the Warrens?"

"Yeah, said Arnie took her in the bathroom with the fan running and the shower on to tell her that he'd been working for them." Cindy banged her hand on her forehead. "I am such an idiot."

"No, come on now. It's been months since he was killed, I would never have guessed that they'd left bugs behind or that anyone was paying any attention to them even if they had. If anything, I'd have thought they snuck in to take them out."

Cindy shivered as she set her fork down. "Still feels creepy that someone was in here. And dammit, I'm going to miss that laptop. It had all of my photography software on it and a ton of my pictures." Luckily, her beautiful new camera was sitting on the kitchen table between them, it's memory card intact. She rested her hand on it as she talked.

"What made you put it in your laundry hamper?" Ray looked up from his food.

Cindy laughed. "No one wants to search through dirty laundry, not even thieves. I grew up in a tough part of the city and our apartment was broken into more than once. My mom used to keep spare cash there, what little she had she'd roll up and tuck into a sock, drop it in the bottom of the hamper."

Ray laughed. "Pretty smart, did you lose a lot of photographs with the computer? Is that where you stored them?"

Cindy shook her head and finished her beer. "No, the other thing my mom taught me about was the importance of a safe-deposit box. When she was a kid, her house burned along with so many of her parents belongings and documents that they had a scary couple of years trying to recover from it. I can remember being a little girl, seeing her standing next to me at the bank as that big, thick metal door opened to reveal the walls of lock boxes. I got in the habit of putting my memory cards in the lock box along with whatever paperwork I cared about."

"Have you ever thought about selling your photographs? I think they're really something."

She smiled in spite of the awful scene around her, thankful that she was finally getting to know this generous man.

"I've toyed with the idea. There's a camera shop I go to regularly," she laughed, "Well, it's a pawn shop actually. But the owner is a great photographer and he got me hooked up with a local photography club. We meet once a month or so, share photographs and critique each other's work. They've actually been encouraging me to look into it, but..." she shrugged."

"But what?"

"I don't know, maybe it's fear or selfishness, a lack of confidence would be the main block I suppose." She shifted and got to her feet, effectively cutting off the line of conversation. She and Ray had cleaned the living room up some before sitting down to eat. The police report had listed the damage but except for the laptop, nothing else seemed to be missing. Now Cindy began clearing away the plates, "I guess I'd better put the bugs in place and get back to cleaning up this mess."

But Ray shook his head and shifted his chair back from the

table. "Come here," he patted his leg and reached out for Cindy's hand once she was close. She felt a little silly but was happy enough to sit down and feel his arms surround her. She held on tight, letting a few tears fall at last.

Ray kept his hand against her back. " Why don't we get things cleaned up and then go back to my place for the night. You can tell our listeners that you don't feel safe here on your own."

CHAPTER SIXTEEN

*F*riday morning Carolyn was just settling down to her desk when her cell phone rang with a familiar tune. "Janine, how are you?"

"I'm good, Carolyn, really good. I've decided to take you up on your offer."

"Yeah! Woohoo! I am literally jumping up and down in my chair. I'm so happy."

"Well, I was hesitant but talking with Sean helped. He and his girlfriend will take care of this place for me. If I decide to stay past the holidays, he and I will have to talk more but for now, we're good. How soon do you want us there?"

"Is tomorrow too soon?" Carolyn could hear her friend's wonderful laugh spilling out of the phone.

"You are crazy, rich girl, do you know that? How about next weekend? That will give me some time to pack and make sure April is settled with the idea too."

"Perfect, I can't wait to see you. I'm going to start getting your rooms ready right this minute."

She heard a caution in her friend's voice then. "Carolyn, are you sure about the art space, you know my canvases are pretty big."

"They're big and beautiful Janine and I promise there will be room for all of them. Just get yourselves here and we'll work it out together."

"Okay, if you say so. I'll give you a call once we're on our way."

"Sounds great, drive safely please!" She hung up the phone and tucked it into her pocket before heading out to find PJ.

This morning, PJ and Rusty were busy with Rupert on the patio outside of the classroom. Carolyn noticed four big boxes lined up on the far side. "Hi guys, what's going on? What's in the boxes?"

"Surpize, Mama, Surpize from Rupert!" PJ was jumping up and down in anticipation. Carolyn looked up at the older man and saw a sly smile spreading across his features.

Rupert shrugged. "I was hoping we'd have it all finished before you noticed but I guess the jig is up." He motioned for Rusty and PJ to join him as he pulled out a small pocketknife and began cutting the plastic straps around the big boxes. "These are a gift from Helen and me. We're so impressed by this school and your plans, we wanted to make a contribution." He tore through the cardboard sides of the first box to reveal a pair of bright red tricycles.

"Yeah! Yeah!" PJ was jumping up and down as they were set upright on the broad patio. He jumped on and was quickly riding circles around the three of them.

"I don't know what to say, Rupert. This is so generous!"

"Wait, there's more!" He laughed and opened up the rest of the big boxes. One held a pair of balance bicycles, the kind without pedals while the last two held small bicycles with pedals and sets of training wheels ready to be installed. "We thought, something for everyone, you know, developmentally. And this way," he gestured toward the patio where she noticed a maze of sorts was being drawn onto the stone tiles.

"Rupert, are you all making a road here? Won't it destroy the tiles?"

"No, no, I checked at the builders' supply place and they assured me that this paint will wear off on its own over the course of a year or two, or we can just clean it off with a power washer." PJ was already following the winding path when Rusty straddled a balance bike and walked his way along behind him. Carolyn and Rupert beamed at the sight of them.

Carolyn laughed, pointing at Rusty, "I think you're going to need a bigger bike, buddy!" He grinned and watched as PJ circled around.

"Actually, I'm going to be the policeman!" He got off the small bike and stood up tall at what appeared to be an intersection. As PJ came up to it, he held his hand out in front of him.

"Stop PJ, it's someone else's turn to go through now." Carolyn watched as the young man effectively, began teaching PJ about the rules of the road. It reminded her of the summer Safety Town programs she taught during college.

"Rusty, I'm really impressed. Would you like to work for my school, helping to watch the children on the playground?"

Rusty looked over at his grandfather before answering. "If Grandpa says it's okay, I'd like that a lot." He looked again at his grandfather.

Rupert's voice caught briefly before he answered, "I think that would be wonderful, Rusty." Carolyn couldn't be sure but she thought his eyes looked a little damp.

She turned to PJ. "This is all so wonderful, I almost forgot my big news. April is coming, PJ!" The little boy jumped off the trike and ran to wrap his arms around Carolyn's legs.

"Really, Mama?" She smiled and leaned over to hug him.

"Yes, really!" She rubbed PJ's back before he ran off to try a different bike. Then she paused to give Rupert a warm hug as well. "You've made me feel so welcome here I don't know how to thank you."

But Rupert just shook his head. "No, Miss, it's you who've made all the difference." He looked over at his grandson as he settled back down to paint. "You have no idea what all of this has meant for Rusty and for Helen and myself. You treat him like a person, Miss, not everyone does that, you know?"

"He's terrific, Rupert, and I think you and Helen deserve all the credit in the world for raising him to be such a fine young man."

Carolyn watched for a few more minutes before going in to talk with Helen about rooms for Janine and April.

A few days later the paint on the play area was dry and PJ was given the go-ahead to ride on it. It had been a difficult morning. Carolyn had made an appointment at the police station to take PJ and have the DNA test. They'd arrived that morning a little before 9:00 and a burly man named Gauthier with a three-day-old beard and jelly on his tie had taken them into a cramped, smelly room to wait. PJ had begun crying almost immediately. Carolyn struggled to calm him.

After nearly twenty-five minutes, the man returned. He took his time looking her up and down pointedly before taking a plastic kit out of a clear, red bag. Carolyn had expected the kind of set up that she'd seen at blood drives with their careful screenings and packaging. This looked more like someone's lunch preparation than a sterile test, but the room was closing in on her and she was eager to get home. She took the swab from him and brushed the inside of her cheek and then reached for the other to do PJ. But the man snatched it out of her reach and barked at the little boy to open his mouth. PJ screamed as the swab was stabbed against his small cheek. Carolyn wanted to lash out at the man, but chose to gather up PJ and leave as quickly as possible. She fumed all the way back home.

Angela had come to stay with PJ for the afternoon and he was eager to take her out to see the new patio design. Carolyn followed along just out of sight, wondering what reaction her mother might have. PJ jumped on the tricycle and began circling Angela at a higher and higher rate of speed until she called out in fear, "Tim,

Tim, slow down!" PJ looked quizzically at her but slowed to a more reasonable speed.

Carolyn leaned against the doorframe, stunned. She took a deep breath and walked out onto the patio. "PJ, are you showing Grandma all of the stops and turns?"

Angela's face went blank for a moment before Carolyn saw the understanding return. Angela walked to stand by Carolyn then. "It's wonderful, Carolyn, how did you come up with this? It's perfect for your little daycare center."

The words 'little daycare center' rankled. A preschool program designed to identify special education students' needs and then integrate them into a regular education program was a bit more than a daycare. Carolyn managed to hold her tongue, though, and answered Angela civilly. "Rupert, Rusty and PJ came up with this. Do you like it?"

Angela watched as PJ careened around a corner and nearly fell off the trike before righting it and turning up the speed again. "Frankly, it seems a little dangerous but I'm sure you know what's best."

Carolyn waited before speaking again. Her mother had always had such a knack for saying something positive while at the same time undercutting it with her disapproving tone. But Carolyn had too much to do that afternoon to stand around worrying about her mother's tone. "Hey, buddy, just a half hour more. Then you and Grandma need to come in." He stuck his lower lip out briefly but nodded his head in agreement.

"Okay mama. Gamma, come walk on our road." He waved his grandmother over and Carolyn took the opportunity to go back inside.

When a storm came up in the late afternoon, Carolyn talked Angela into staying for dinner and overnight again. They all met in the kitchen where Rusty was setting plates out and PJ was distributing napkins. It was a relaxed, family type of meal, with beef stew and biscuits that Helen pulled from the oven just as they were sitting down. Carolyn noticed that her mother seemed more quiet than usual, but PJ was happily trying to tell a long story about a cartoon he had seen so she didn't pay it a lot of attention. After the meal, she and PJ walked with Angela down the long hallway to their rooms. She watched Angela step into the guest room and then continued to the bathroom to start the tub for PJ.

PJ seemed to go back and forth between loving and hating having baths. Luckily, tonight he was loving it and she didn't push him to get out until the water was starting to chill. She rubbed him dry with a soft towel and got him into a pair of ninja turtle pajamas. "Time for PJ's, PJ," always got a laugh from him. She peeked in the guest room to see if Angela would like to read him a bedtime story, but her mother had already dozed off. So she and PJ continued down the hallway to his room and climbed into the big armchair by his bed to read stories. When he began to yawn, she helped him into his big-boy bed and pulled the blankets up one by one. He was nearly asleep by the time the last one was in place.

Carolyn closed his door and walked back toward the room her mother was using but when she looked in, her mother was nowhere to be seen. She checked the bathroom and her own room next door but still didn't find her. The hall ended in the suite of rooms that had been Edward's, so that end of the hallway was dark. Carolyn checked it briefly anyway but still didn't find Angela so she moved in the opposite direction, back toward the lights of the kitchen and living room. She heard an odd sound then, a whimpering sort of cry and she found Helen crouched in front of a big armchair where Angela was curled up into a ball, covering her eyes and refusing to talk. Helen stepped back and nodded to Carolyn who took her place on the floor in front of the chair.

"Mom, what's wrong? Are you hurt?"

Her mother snarled in answer, "Who are you? Why are you keeping me here? I want to go home!"

Carolyn was taken aback by the anger in her mother's voice. She tried to keep her tone even. "Mom, it's me, your daughter, Carolyn, you're here because of the storm."

Her mother threw her hands out in front of her and started to stand but lightning flashed outside the window and she withdrew into a tighter ball. "I don't have a daughter. What are you talking about? Let me go home!"

Carolyn sat back on the floor, shocked by the statement. Then she leaned forward and rested her hand on her mother's knee but Angela brushed it off and withdrew again. "Mom, I'm Carolyn, your daughter, remember? You were watching my son PJ this afternoon."

Angela lashed out again, "I don't have a daughter. Carolyn, what kind of a stupid name is that? You don't even look like a girl."

Carolyn had no idea what to say to that so she sat back on the floor and waited. She watched as fatigue gradually took the place of her mother's anger. Her eyelids began drooping and she shivered. Carolyn stood then and offered her hand to her mother. She used the gentlest tone that she could. "Mom, you're tired and cold, let me take you back to your bedroom." She was surprised when Angela stood up willingly and walked with her down the long hallway. Carolyn kept one arm loosely draped over her shoulder and with the other, held her mother's hand. When they got to the bedroom, she helped her mother into the nightgown that she'd bought to have on hand. She waited as her mother went in to the adjacent bathroom. After she had used the bathroom and brushed her teeth, she came out and settled easily under the covers. Carolyn watched as Angela fell asleep almost as quickly as PJ had.

When she'd waited for about 10 minutes, Carolyn stole quietly out of the room, grateful that a small night-light was in place near the door. She shut the door and then leaned against it, trying to keep tears from falling. She jumped when a hand touched her on the shoulder but it was just Helen and the two of them walked back to the kitchen together.

"My god, Helen, what was that? *'I don't have a daughter, Carolyn is a stupid name'*?" She shook her head and sat down at the small table where Helen had set out a pot of tea and a few pretzels.

"Rupert and I had a friend years ago, who would become frightened and disoriented in the evening like that. The doctor called it 'sundowning'. Apparently it happens a lot in senior centers."

"What do I do? How can I help her if she doesn't even know me?"

Helen poured her a cup of tea and handed her the plastic bear filled with honey. "I don't think you can do anything about it, except get her through the night and then call her doctor in the morning."

Carolyn sat back, the cup of tea held close to her chest. Then she heard the door to her mother's bedroom open and she went to meet her. Throughout the night, she re-settled her mother back in bed three or four times, never really sleeping in between as she listened for the sounds of her restlessness. She didn't think she'd ever been so glad to see the sun come up before.

In the morning, Carolyn persuaded her mother to stay and play with PJ a bit longer. And after talking with Dr. Gilbert's secretary, she was on the phone with her brother. "It was so weird, Curt, she said Carolyn was a stupid name for a girl!"

"Well, I always thought..."

"This is no time for joking around! It scared me to death! We have to do something. It's not safe for her to be at home anymore."

"Well, you may have the money it takes to pay for a nursing home for her, but I sure don't."

Carolyn sagged back into her desk chair. "I don't want to put her in a nursing home, do you?"

"Well no, but what choice do we have? You can probably afford one of the nicer ones."

Carolyn looked around the library at the beautiful room with its walls of books and wide windows. If Helen and Rupert were willing to stand it, she guessed she'd have to try it too. "Listen, I'm willing to have her here, but I don't want her freaking out on me again. Dr. Gilbert's secretary said that the more familiar and routine we make her surroundings, the better it will be. I have a room for her but tomorrow I want you to go and gather up whatever you can from her house. I think she'll be reassured if her own belongings are where she can see them."

Curt hesitated. Carolyn knew that he was angry at having to leave work again to deal with all of this. But he would have to admit Carolyn was taking on the lion's share of it all so it was more than fair of her to ask this of him. "I'll see what I can do. I think Brenda's free to help me too."

"That would be great. I'm hoping Mom and I can see Dr. Gilbert tomorrow morning. I want her help in breaking the news to her."

"That's going to be a tough sell."

"You're telling me. You and Brenda should plan to stay for dinner too."

"Well, we'll see how it goes."

CHAPTER SEVENTEEN

*A*s September turned into October, the campground population ebbed and flowed and then gradually began to diminish. Both the cooler weather and the growing quiet suited Greg as he spent his days helping the volunteers, walking the trails and making his small meals. One morning he found himself taking a wide step onto a wobbling kayak that a late summer tourist had left behind. The small dock felt steady under his right foot but the left one was uncertain at best. He gasped as the boat lurched a few inches, then held his breath as he dared to shift his weight and draw the other foot into the boat. Once in, he crouched low, trying to find the proper balance before inching his butt onto the metal seat. At least he knew how to swim, he told himself.

As a city boy, Greg had taken lessons each year at the local YMCA pool, but he'd never experienced water this way. It had already taken him several weeks to learn how to swim out in the surf the way the tourists did. He watched as they jumped and played in the waves, body surfing toward shore in ways he'd never imagined. He prided himself on being a fairly good body surfer now, as long as it wasn't too rough. But boating, even in a small kayak like this, that was another step altogether.

Determined, he slowly bent and picked up the double-ended paddle, unhooked the loop of rope from the rusty cleat and gently pushed himself away from the low dock. The kayak wobbled beneath him and he sucked in another big breath before it righted itself and carried him gently away from the shore. He smiled as he caught sight of a young girl playing at the water's edge. She smiled back with a wide grin that was missing a couple of teeth and Greg made a quick wave with the end of his paddle. Since it was a state park, the waterways were all marked and he was able to move between the small barrier islands without worrying that he'd get lost. For his first voyage out, he stuck closely to the shoreline, learning slowly about how to paddle and steer without toppling out of the small boat. After just half an hour he was tired and a slight ache was forming between his shoulder blades, but he also felt a sense of accomplishment and for that he was grateful. Each day after that he made a point of going out farther and farther. He stayed well away from the ocean side of the island as the waves could be unpredictable, but finally he was able to row through the channels all the way to the mainland and back.

When he first arrived, Greg had been surprised to find that the island had cell phone service and with a cheap model phone he was able to use the Internet for short periods. Electrical power was more of an issue than reception. The volunteer staff had grown to trust him and left the key where he could access it easily, so he'd developed a system where he charged the phone and laptop in the park's concession stand well after dark. He found the buzz of insects around the light and the scrufflings of small animals outside the door, an odd sort of company, especially after all his years of city living. The screech of birds in the night could still send a chill through him, but mostly he'd learned to tune it all out. Once a week or so he rode the ferry across to the lot where his car was continuing to rust in its effort to return to the earth. It kept starting for him, though, a small blessing.

He tried to vary his movements each week, a different time, a different direction, but in this relatively quiet area of the state there weren't a whole lot of choices. He usually sought out the produce stands and smaller groceries, paying cash as he went. One Sunday, not long after he'd found the park, he'd taken the time to drive to the far side of Jacksonville, to a small branch bank where he was able to withdraw the rest of his funds. He'd waited until the tellers were busy with a long line of customers before stepping up and taking care of the transaction. Then, he'd driven an elaborate route around the town, detouring toward the South Carolina border before returning north on a small two lane road that turned into dirt before connecting back with the state road system. He knew it was a risk, but his last paycheck had run out and he felt that he didn't have any choice. Afterwards he'd stocked up on supplies and not left the island again for nearly two weeks.

One piece of luck had fallen into his lap, though. As August drew to a close, the number of volunteers on the island dwindled and the young man who'd been running the small concession stand, had returned to college. The ferryboat captain, noting Greg's prolonged stay on the island, had recommended him for the sole, paid position. It was just minimum wage for a few hours a week but it was enough to keep him going. Again he'd been able to use a false name and arrange to be paid in cash. Greg figured someone above him was making a little extra on the side but it didn't matter to him. He could ride the ferry for free without having to check in or be counted and that suited his needs as well. Mostly, when he sat behind the quiet counter listening to the waves breaking and the wind moving through the trees, he liked to think of Arnie, to picture him as a gangly young man, chatting with the tourists, his wonderful laugh spilling over their heads.

CHAPTER EIGHTEEN

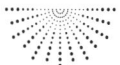

*V*ince and Tony seemed happy enough staying at the safe house. Hell, Pete thought, James would probably have them moved into that control center house by now if he intended to use them as muscle. Damn, for an ornery, fat old slob, the man had moved fast. There he was living it up in Walt's house, lording it over the peons left behind in Jay's wake. Well, Pete wanted nothing to do with all that, or as little as possible at least. Once he'd finally gotten back to the neighborhood from overseas, he'd found himself a tiny, one bedroom apartment over a pizza joint. It was loud and stunk of old cheese most of the time, but at least it was private. He snagged a parking space out on the street and carried his bag and the agent's laptop up to his room. He took a few minutes to inspect everything, checking for any bugs or booby traps that might have been left, but he found nothing. Since the car explosion, he'd become a helluva lot more cautious.

Once satisfied that his place was untouched, he got a beer from the refrigerator and set up the laptop on his small kitchen table. He was happy to find it was almost fully charged since he hadn't bothered to swipe the cord with it. He planned to search it and then toss it, or rather sell it to some dimwit. He paid no attention to the stunning, skyline shot that was her screen's wall paper, but thought instead, what a sap, she didn't even have it password protected. He shook his head as he began clicking on various icons from the desktop. It soon became apparent though, that the agent kept nothing from her work on the laptop. Except for some word files and a bill paying spreadsheet, the unit was almost entirely devoted to her photography. Pete found himself looking through several files of pictures and was impressed enough to change his mind about the device. He wasn't going to just toss it, first he was going to sell those images and make some money off the bitch.

He left it and went in search of another beer and the half a sandwich he'd left yesterday. If he got hungry later, he could always call downstairs for something else. But in the meantime, he turned on the TV, flipped through the channels until he found a football game, and settled on the couch. He kept thinking back to the kid with the headset and what he'd said about the accountant Lowe. Funny, he wasn't surprised to hear about Hanes, but he'd never gotten any kind of homosexual vibe from Lowe. Lowe's wife was a fox too, from what he'd seen that day. What in the hell?

God he hated fags. Fucking monsters as far as he was concerned. Now they were every goddamn where, on TV, in the news, at the damned grocery where he shopped. He'd been just 22 when he went to prison for the first time. Twenty-two and skinny as hell, his cellmate had taken one look at him and used him from the very first night. Pete knew he'd screamed his head off but no one in there had given a rat's ass about the latest punk to arrive. Two years it had taken him to put on enough meat and muscle to shove the guy's head in the toilet. Then he'd run the joint, shopped inmates for money and drugs and never taken shit from anyone again.

Forcing himself to shift his thinking, he focused in on Hanes and Lowe, knowing the combination of the two could be an issue. With the accountant gone, what exactly did Hanes know? More importantly, though, where could he be? Pete reached over to grab his own laptop and the set of headphones resting on top. He'd have a listen in on the agent's apartment and see where to go from there. He didn't have the high quality bugs that James was running, but he figured his would be good enough.

He settled the headphones on his ears and connected to the bug in the living room. When the sound came through, it blasted a roaring sound in his ears and he whipped the headphones off. Goddamn, what in the hell was that? He listened to the noise without putting the headphones back on and was able to recognize the sound of a vacuum cleaner. Well shit, of course she was cleaning up the mess he'd made. It seemed to take forever, though, and he'd fallen asleep to the noise and the football game. The sound cut off then suddenly, and the quiet woke him.

"I guess that's all I can do tonight. Thanks again for helping. I'll just pack a small bag and follow you in my car. I'll come back in the morning before work and finish the clean up." He heard the voices move away from the bug toward what he thought was the bedroom but apparently that one wasn't working. He didn't pick up any other sound until he heard water running. The kitchen, he figured, but then footsteps moved from one room through the living room until he heard the outer door close. Oh well, he'd pick it up in the morning. Pete tossed the empty beer cans into the recycle bag under his sink and wiped down the counter one more time. No fucking way was he going to live like those disgusting Morelli brothers. He checked his locks one more time and turned in for the night. He set his laptop on the floor by his bed so that it could recharge, then turned the unit's sound on so that he could hear the agent when she returned in the morning.

An incredibly loud grinding sound woke him. He looked around the room, his eyes catching on the 5:43 of the bedside clock. Then he spotted the laptop and reached to hit the mute button. He waited for a few minutes and then turned the sound back on. The grinding had stopped but water was running and there was little he could hear over that. Shit, he should have bought better equipment. But money was tight. He listened again and this time, some sort of morning TV program seemed to be blaring on about the day's weather. He turned the sound down lower and tried to get back to sleep.

When he awoke again his clock read 7:30 and the laptop was silent. Shit, she must have left for work while he was sleeping. He took a quick shower, ate half of an old bagel and dressed for the day. His plan was to go check Greg Hanes's apartment, see if there was anything there to find. He took the time to put on a sport coat and tie in case he had to deal with a landlord or somebody in order to get into the apartment.

Hanes's apartment wasn't too far so Pete elected to walk. The outer door was locked but another tenant was exiting as he walked up and held the door open. Shit, people got what they deserved in this world. What the fuck's the point of having a locked outer door if you're going to let in any schmuck that walks up? He expected to slip through Hanes's door with just his credit card, but there were two additional locks. He glanced around the hallway before pulling out a slim tool case and jimmying first one and then the other. He stepped into the dark room and closed the door behind him. There was a stale quality to the air that told him no one had been there in quite some time. Dust lay in a thick coat on the kitchen table and chairs. He opened the fridge and then shut it quickly but the smell of rotten lunchmeat had already spilled out into the room. Pete pulled a dishtowel out of a drawer and held it to his nose. He moved toward the back bedroom. Several of the dresser drawers were hanging open but nearly empty. A glass dish of coins appeared to have broken and was left on the floor near the bed. Pete noted the nice TV mounted to the wall and wondered briefly what he could get for it, but that felt like too much of a hassle, especially since he'd walked. He searched through the bedside table and the closet but found nothing. He gave the bathroom a quick look before returning to the living room.

The smell was still strong but he spotted a desk against the far wall. Again, several drawers had been left hanging open. He sat and pulled out a few files from the bottom drawer but he was trying to hold his breath and didn't have the patience to go through more than a handful of them. Shit, there was nothing here. Clearly Hanes had left in a hurry and been gone a long time. He tried to remember what he knew about Hanes but he hadn't had a lot to do with him. Jay had said that there was a place that Hanes and Lowe met to make their cash exchanges. Where had that been?

Pete began walking home and was glad of the sport coat as a cold wind began to pick up. He was racking his brain trying to remember what Jay had said. He considered calling up Vince or Tony to find out if either of them remembered but he really didn't want to do that. He was nearly back at his own front door when he remembered. It was Lulu's.

At six, he was seated at the bar at Lulu's with the talkative bartender, CB. It sure hadn't taken much to get him going. "Wow, I can't believe how everyone keeps asking about those two guys."

"Everybody?" Pete adopted a friendly smile and waited for the bartender to take the bait.

"Yea, good looking FBI agent was in asking just recently, trying to figure out who killed the one guy, I guess. You on that too?" CB kept up with his work as he talked, clearing plates and wiping down the bar.

Pete nearly choked on his beer. He'd been the fucking driver, for God's sake. He took out his handkerchief and pretended to blow his nose as he weighed what to say. He finally stuffed it back into his pants pocket and tried to adopt a nonchalant tone of voice. "No, not me. I just owe the guy Hanes some money, trying to find him, see if I have to pay him back or not," he grinned, "you know?"

CB nodded. "Not planning to look too hard, I guess, huh?"

"You got that right," Pete laughed and settled into eating his meal. The food wasn't half bad, he decided, sure beat the pizza they were making over at his place. He'd check in on the agent once he got back home, might have to step up his game in that area, he thought. She was the only lead he had.

CHAPTER NINETEEN

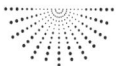

*I*t was still dark in the morning and rather cold when Cindy let herself back into her apartment. She hated leaving Ray's warm bed so early but she'd forgotten the shoes she needed for work and decided she might as well have breakfast at her own place. Once they'd finished picking up the night before, they had replaced two of the listening devices, one in the kitchen and one in the living room. She'd taken a special delight in running the vacuum cleaner over and over in the area near one of the bugs before packing up and leaving. This morning she happily ran her coffee grinder through two cycles next to the kitchen bug before turning on her TV and sitting down to eat. She hated morning TV, but was eager to create as much noise as she could. She ate a bowl of cold cereal as she flipped through her cell phone and located the information she needed to file the insurance claim. With the TV blaring she took another careful look around her apartment before putting on her shoes and leaving for the day. She flipped off the TV and prayed that whoever it was would lose interest in her place.

It took most of the morning for her to clear the various chores that had collected in her in-box. The Warren case was involving a big part of the office but other cases were going on as well and her computer skills were needed in a variety of them. Finally, she and Ray met for lunch around one at the cafe on the corner.

"So how'd it go at your place this morning?" Ray asked around a mouthful of sandwich.

Cindy was sipping at her coke, an indulgence that she allowed herself twice a week. She knew something that could clean a car battery couldn't be good for her but it was a habit she just couldn't break. She laughed as she told Ray about running the coffee grinder and the TV. They finished their lunches and before long were making their way back along the busy sidewalk. Once they were inside, they settled at Ray's desk. "I've carved out some time this afternoon for us to work on this. Where do you think we should start? Do you have any idea who in the Warren organization could be interested in me?"

Ray rested his glasses on his head. "Well everyone would be interested if they knew you like I do." He wiggled his eyebrows and Cindy laughed.

"That's not what I meant." She had no interest in being caught blushing in the work place.

"Okay, Okay." He glanced at his chicken scratched notes and gave her a report of what he'd learned that morning. "So I asked around the office and there are still agents watching a number of the players in the Warren organization. James Warren, Walt's younger brother, has taken up residence in Walt's old home and he's installed a bunch of lackeys at his place in the western borough." He motioned over his shoulder, "A couple of guys spotted the Morelli brothers going into the place yesterday at the same time as, wait for it..." He drummed his forefingers on the edge of the desk.

"Pete Turner."

"Right you are! It sounds like he arrived there about an hour after you left the widow's house."

"So you think he's the one who wrecked my apartment."

Ray shrugged. "It's anyone's guess at this point. But, it is confirmation that he's back and possibly working for them again."

"So what's our next step?"

Ray set his glasses on the table. "I've been looking at financial reports for the last hour and you've probably had your nose stuck in your computer all morning, want to get out of here for a little while?"

Cindy stood, happily slipping back into her coat. "Sounds great, where do you think we should go?"

Ray folded his glasses and tucked them into his shirt pocket before putting his old Steeler's jacket on as well. "I want to go and get a look at Hanes's apartment. It's probably a long shot, but who knows?"

The drive took nearly an hour as they sat in traffic. They parked and found the outer door of the building locked, so they rang the super's apartment and waited to be let in. An indifferent man, he let them into the unit without even looking at their ID's. Ray and Cindy stepped into the apartment and clapped their hands over their noses. "Geez, what is that?" The smell was biting. They quickly stepped away from the kitchen where it seemed strongest.

"Ray, look." Cindy opened a drape and in the sunlight it was easy to see the layers of dust around the place but also, where the dust had been disturbed. "Someone's been here before us." They drew their weapons as a precaution but saw nothing out of order in the rest of the apartment. They holstered them and Cindy sat down at the desk. The lower drawer was still ajar and a few files were scattered on top of the desk. "Looks like someone had a quick look here, not very thorough, though," she noted as she set the few open files aside and reached back into the drawer. She took the time to page through the others slowly, client information was what most seemed to contain. A separate folder held billing information and she handed that one to Ray to look through. He spread it out on the dusty coffee table and began going over the pages. The last folder in the drawer was a fat, misshapen one that held what looked like nearly a hundred photographs. Cindy returned all of the other files to the drawer and then began looking through the photographs, mostly surveillance shots. She saw grainy pictures of men with women who did not appear to be wife material, someone walking with a thick cane and then the picture of health swinging a golf club.

Toward the back of the file the pictures seemed to be a little older and more personal. There were several that appeared to be from Hanes's college days, friends decked out in Penn State colors at a football game and a Halloween party. She looked for Marybeth Rogers in the photos but realized they must have been taken after she left the college and went into the witness protection program. Finally, she looked again into the open drawer and saw a folded photograph that seemed to have slipped into the seam of the drawer. She pulled it out and spread it open in front of her. "Ray, look at this."

The photograph showed Arnie Lowe, his wife Pamela and their two daughters in front of a brown state park sign. The girls were quite small so she knew the picture was an old one. What caught at her though, was the way it had been folded. It had been carefully creased between Arnie and his wife so that she and the children were folded behind and a laughing Arnie remained looking out. Ray leaned against the desk and took the photograph from Cindy. "Just makes me sad, you know? I got the feeling from interviewing Marybeth that Greg is a really nice guy. Seems like he deserves more than just half a photograph, you know?"

Cindy nodded in agreement. "Do you think we're putting him in more danger by looking for him? Maybe he's trying to make a new life away from all of this." She gestured at the low rent apartment around her, the solitary nature of the place so obvious even in disuse.

Ray shrugged. "I don't know, but here's my worry. Marybeth

went looking for her daughter because she thought Jay Warren was dead and she assumed she was safe. Maybe Hanes feels now that Jay's in jail, it's finally safe for him." Then he gestured at the streaks through the dust, "but clearly, it's not as safe as he thinks." He handed the photograph back to Cindy and replaced the bill folder in the drawer. "I still think his best chance is with us. At least we care about his safety."

Cindy rose, examined the folded photograph again and then tucked it into her pocket. "The widow talked about a place on the North Carolina coast where the family used to go for vacations. Let me see what I can find out from this photograph."

They closed the door behind them and waited for the super to re-lock it.

"Gonna have to clear it out, he doesn't come back soon, you know?"

"How soon?" Ray asked, wondering if there was anything they could or should do about it. The super shook out an old handkerchief and blew his nose loudly. "End of the year, I suppose. Lease runs out then so I won't have much choice. You two interested in renting it?"

Ray and Cindy shook their heads.

CHAPTER TWENTY

*I*t turned out to be two days before the meeting with Dr. Gilbert could be arranged. Carolyn had driven her mother home in the morning, reluctant to leave her and Curt had postponed picking up her things until the next day. She called to check on her mother several times and was there early the following morning for the meeting. Her mother was clear and lucid and absolutely furious at the idea of leaving her home. She alternated between blaming Carolyn and pleading with the doctor. But Dr. Gilbert had remained both firm and reassuring and Angela had been forced to acquiesce.

Back in the car, Carolyn put her hand on her mother's shoulder and spoke gently. "I'm worried about you, Mom. I don't want anything to happen to you."

Angela remained stiff-backed but she spoke without anger. "I know that, dear. I know you mean well, but giving up my freedom, it's such a hard thing." She shook her head back and forth. "I just don't see the need. I know I forget things once in a while. I just don't know why you're all making such a big stink. Everyone forgets things when they get older."

Carolyn kept her voice soft but firm. "I know it's hard, but let's just see how it goes. We won't take any big steps until we get a better sense of what's going on. For now, let's go to your house and pack a bag and then Curt can bring over some of your other things. We'll take it from there."

Angela nodded, then shut her eyes as Carolyn turned on the car. They made the drive in good time, collected her things and were back in time to sit down to lunch with PJ. Seeing him brightened her mother's spirits and they went off exploring after the meal.

Back in her office, Carolyn sat down to work but was interrupted almost immediately by her cell phone.

"Carolyn, it's Charlie. Do you have a minute?"

"Sure Charlie, what's up?" She fiddled with the computer, opening her email.

"Dear, I don't know how to say this."

Carolyn sat up straight. The tone of voice was chilling. "Are you all right?"

"I'm fine dear but I'm afraid we have a problem with the DNA test. A sergeant from the police station just called to tell me that the samples from you and PJ don't match Jay Warren."

Carolyn was stunned. "What do you mean? What about the other samples we sent, the ones we were having compared to Edward Clark's DNA?"

"I'm afraid we haven't gotten those results back yet. Private labs can take longer, especially since we're asking for more than just a paternity test."

"So what does this mean?" She stood and walked toward the wall of windows, frightened for what might come next. "What should I do? We've set the open house for two weeks from now with a soft start before that. Do I need to cancel everything?"

"Now, now, let's not get ahead of ourselves here. I'm going to contact the lab doing our tests and see what I can find out. I'm also going to talk with our lawyers to see what they recommend. I just felt like I needed to give you a heads up, is all."

Carolyn returned to her desk and flopped down in her chair. "Wow, I don't even know what to think, Charlie. All of a sudden it feels like I've been building a house of cards, not something substantial like I thought."

"Now, don't give up on me here kiddo, remember, my faith is still in you. We'll figure this out. Just give me a little bit of time."

"All right, Charlie, if you're sure. I'm meeting tomorrow with your friend to finish the plans for the open house. I'll do my best to keep the cost down but if I need to pull the plug, you've got to tell me as soon as you can."

"I know dear, I know. I'll talk with you soon."

Carolyn hung up the phone but sat in her chair unmoving. What had she done? Her mother was here now. Janine would be here by the weekend, had she just upset all of those lives for nothing? She was about to bury her head in her hands when her cell phone rang again.

It was an unfamiliar number so she almost let it go, but then, she remembered she was trying to start a business. Perhaps it was the parent of a child calling. She summoned up her best voice. "Edward Clark Children's Center, how may I help you?"

"Caro, it's Alex, How's it going? I'm back in town."

My God, if it wasn't one damn thing it was another. She had to admit that she was still moved by the sound of his voice, but today in particular, she had no idea what to say. She felt bad knowing her tone was not welcoming.

"Is this a bad time?"

"Uh, kind of." She thought, here was one more person uprooting their life just to follow her cockamamie scheme. The number of people that she was going to be letting down if this failed, felt staggering. "Did you have a good trip?"

"It was easy enough. I've got a place now, and once I get everything moved in, I wanted to see about having PJ over. Would you be okay with that?"

Carolyn couldn't help but picture the joy she'd seen on PJ's face at their picnic as he sat on Alex's lap. She tried for a friendlier tone. "Sure, Alex, I think PJ would love to spend time with you."

"Great, listen, could I pick him up on Friday, say around three? Could he sleep over, too? I've got a room just for him that I'm fixing up."

Carolyn hesitated. "He hasn't slept over anywhere before Alex, so I'm not sure about the first visit. Why don't you give him time to get used to your new place," and you, she thought. She worried that Alex would be offended but his response was just the opposite and she couldn't help but be relieved.

"That sounds perfect, Carolyn, ease him into it. Makes sense to me." Carolyn wanted to curl up in a big ball by the fireplace. Instead, she left the phone on the desk and went to work in her classroom.

The atrium was turning out better than she had anticipated. Light spilling in through the tall windows made it an inviting room even on a chilly day. The week before she had finished the classroom area and the reading nook where pillows and low benches nestled under one of the big windows. She had hung a series of low bookshelves and filled them with many of PJ's picture books and others that she had found at a garage sale and online. As she finished arranging the last books and pillows she felt a deep sense of satisfaction begin to replace the annoyance that the morning had brought on.

Pleased with the space, Carolyn moved on from the reading nook to the sunny art area. At the same garage sale, she had found two low tables. She had cleaned and sanded them before turning them over to Rupert and Rusty for painting. Now they had a shiny, black finish that she hoped would prove easy to clean and fairly indestructible. Their drawers would be perfect for small paintbrushes, scissors and whatever else Janine would come up with. She set about assembling the two, double sided easels that would sit on top.

As she worked, Carolyn couldn't help but hear Alex's voice in her head. Before he'd shown up at the house, the last time she'd seen him had been nearly six months ago. They met in the conference room at the lawyers' office and took less than half an hour to divide up their belongings and sign the paperwork completing the divorce. How had all of that become so easy, she wondered? Even now she could see Alex's face that day, drawn and quiet, embarrassed even she thought, but he was still the strikingly handsome man that she had fallen in love with. Her summer flirtation with Janine's brother Sean had been exciting but brief. She thought she was ready for someone new, ready to move forward but somehow it hadn't felt right being in someone else's arms, and sweet as Sean was, he deserved more than she was capable of at that point. Now, as she pictured PJ visiting with Alex in some low rent bachelor's apartment, a shiver went through her. It didn't seem right or fair, somehow, as she looked at the beautiful room around her. Why was she holding back on telling Alex about the money?

CHAPTER TWENTY-ONE

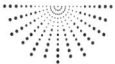

*P*ete had spent a boring evening searching for something to watch on TV and waiting for sound on the agent's laptop. He'd heard her come in but then it had gone quiet. He thought she was still there, maybe in the bedroom or bathroom, but alone, she wasn't making much noise. He checked the tracker he'd put on her car but sure enough, it was still in place at the apartment. He was getting ready to head out to a nearby bar just to break the monotony, when his cell phone buzzed. The caller ID read Helena, Montana but he answered it anyway just for kicks.

"Pete's mortuary and out house" he announced into the phone.

"Cut the shit, moron. I need you to do something for me tomorrow." James practically spit into the phone and Pete thought he could hear him chewing on the other end.

"What do you need?"

"Jay and I are looking at coming into some property here real soon and I want you to go and check it out."

"What kind of property, where?"

"It's a fucking palace over in Hartwood Manor. I'll text you the address."

"How am I supposed to get into some place like that? What do you want to know about it?"

"I want photographs, asshole, I told you, I'm going to own it soon. I want to see what it looks like, see if I'm going to like it. What's it matter to you? Take the goddamn pictures and send them to me." The phone clicked off before Pete could respond. Then a text arrived with an address. Pete went to his laptop and used a real estate app to pull up the address. It sure as hell looked like a palace or a fortress, he thought. How in the world would he get in there?

Saturday morning he showered and shaved, then took the time to iron a white shirt and some pants. He burned himself in the process and was fuming by the time he got into the car. He had fixed a small camera to the lapel of his jacket and tested the camera trigger in his pocket. The real estate ad had given him the idea of posing as a building inspector. He could tell that the listing had recently changed hands so he was planning to twist that to suit his story.

A smooth, circular drive brought him to the front of the house where a wide set of doors stood as his first challenge. He stepped out of the car and smoothed the jacket down, taking a few shots of the impressive entrance. He rang the bell and was surprised when a beautiful young woman opened one of the middle panels. He gave a slight bow and reached his hand out toward her. "Zeke Jones, ma'am, how're you?"

The young woman offered her hand in return but released the grip quickly. "May I help you?"

He pulled out a small flip wallet and flashed a fake ID card without giving her time to study it. "I'm with the city building inspector's office, ma'am. It's our understanding that this property changed hands recently without any proper inspections being done."

Apparently flustered, the woman tucked her hands into the

pockets of her sweatshirt and looked behind her to see if anyone was nearby. As she hesitated, Pete spoke quickly.

"It won't take long, ma'am, just need to do a quick walk around is all, get the lay of the place so to speak." He made a sweeping gesture with his arm. "Seems silly with a place as grand as this but you know how the city can be."

"Well, if you must." Pete had the impression that the big house was empty as she stepped aside and allowed him to enter the foyer. With quick steps she then embarked on a tour of the front part of the house including the library and sitting room before taking him down another wing. He stopped when he saw the brightly painted room.

"What's this?" He paused before walking purposely into the classroom.

"We're getting ready to open a pre-school here and this is our classroom." She hesitated a moment before asking, "Do you have any children or grandchildren Mr. Jones?"

Pete didn't recognize the name he'd given or even notice that she had asked him a question. All he could think was, what the hell would James be doing with a school.

"Mr. Jones?" Carolyn raised her voice.

"I am so sorry Miss, this is such a delightful place. I just lost track there for a minute." He snapped off a number of shots before following her through another wing of the house. By that time, he was bored and figured he had more than enough photographs for James, whatever the fuck he was planning. The young woman was talking again but he stopped in the central area before she could drag him down yet another hallway.

Near the door she stepped back to make more room between them but found herself trapped by a long table. Pete noticed that she stood as tall as she could and said "excuse me" in a tone which apparently she thought would alert him to the situation and cause him to step back. But Pete liked the discomfort he saw on her face and chose to stand there a moment longer than necessary before turning aside. "I believe I've seen enough," he said as he snapped another photo, this time of Carolyn. "I thank you for your time, Miss." He thought that he heard someone coming from the dining area behind him so he walked quickly to the door and escaped back to his car.

Once he got home, Pete downloaded the photographs and was preparing to send them when he reconsidered. He knew he'd learn a hell of a lot more about what was going on if he took them to James in person. So he loaded them onto a small drive, got back into his car and headed for James.

"Got your photographs here for you, boss. What is this place?" The small drive seemed to disappear into James wide paw and indeed he fumbled it, unable to insert it correctly into the desktop computer. Pete noted another huge plastic soda cup but at least the food wrappers had been cleared away. "May I?" He took the drive back, came around the desk and inserted it into the USB port, then stood watching as the images began to appear. James clicked fairly quickly through the images until the atrium classroom appeared. He looked at Pete, "what the fuck is this?"

Pete shrugged. "Looks like a little school to me. So what?"

"So what?" James bellowed. "What kind of an idiot would fuck up a mansion like that by putting a school inside?" He yelled again, this time at the young woman who had appeared in the doorway. "Get that bitch lawyer on the phone for me now! I want to know what the fuck is going on with my property." At that moment he seemed to notice Pete again and gestured for him to go back around the desk.

Pete retreated, but given James's level of agitation, he chose to stand rather than sit. "What do you need here, boss?" It grated on him to refer to the man that way but Pete knew better, at least for now, "Who's the woman?"

"What are you talking about?"

"Page through to the end of the photos, who's the woman?"

James clicked through the photographs until he spotted Carolyn, then he let out a laugh that was more derision than humor. "That's the bitch that thinks she's Jay's daughter. Clark turned Jay's inheritance over to her just before he died. Bitch has no idea who she's messing with, though. We'll have her ass out of that place before the snow flies, just wait."

"Anything I can do?"

"Nah," James picked up the soda cup and gestured toward the door. "I already got the DNA shit sewn up so I'm good."

"I noticed a sign that was being painted. They're having an Open House there next Thursday evening if you want to check it out yourself."

James looked up, a hungry expression on his face. "What time?"

"Seven o'clock, looked like to me." James nodded but said nothing else. Instead, he reached into a lower desk drawer and pulled out a wad of bills, then peeled a couple of hundreds off the outside of the roll. "Stay close to your phone in case I need you, got it?"

Pete took the money and folded it, tucked it in his pocket as he turned to leave. "You know it!" Then he paused and risked a question. "You heard anything from Smokey?

"Who the hell is Smokey?"

Pete waved his hand dismissively. "Ah, just someone else that worked for Jay. Probably dead by now I guess. Take it easy." Pete tried for a casual sort of wave and left the room. He took the stairs down quickly. He thought about stopping by Lulu's again to see if the big bartender had remembered anything else, but it seemed doubtful so he continued on home. Downstairs, he waited a few minutes for them to wrap up a pizza and small salad, then carried it up to his apartment. The place was still untouched so he set up his laptop, grabbed a beer, his last one he noted, and settled down to work. First, he dialed Tony Morelli. It seemed to ring forever but just as he was about to give up, an out of breath voice answered "what?"

"Tony, Pete here. Can you give me Smokey's number?"

"Sure thing, is he around?"

He rattled off the number and Pete made a quick note of it, "I owe you."

"Hey, you got any work for us? James just has us doing this chicken shit stuff, you know, collections, busting knees. We're used to a little more action than that, if you know what I mean."

"Sure, I'll give you a call if I get something lined up. Later." Pete hung up quickly, logged Smokey's number into his phone and then hit dial. This time the phone was answered before the first ring.

"Yeah, who's this?"

"Smokey, Pete Turner here, how you doing?"

"Who the fuck is Pete Turner? Where'd you get this number?"

Pete ran his hand through his hair in frustration. "I worked with Jay Warren. We met up on the docks there in Philly last time a shipment came in."

"Oh wait, didn't I hear you were dead, man?" He laughed. "Sorry about that. Listen, what is up with you guys? I had a whole shipment of bitches come in last week, had to turn 'em over to some local dudes, hoping to move up, if you know what I mean. What's the story there?"

"Just taking a little while getting everything set back up here, you know? Listen, when's the next shipment due in? I want it man, what've you got?"

Smokey was an aging mobster like Pete, a skinny, bald guy, kind of twitchy with a cigarette always tucked above his ear. He reminded Pete more of a junky than a businessman. "Well, if it's a good sized shipment of drugs you want, I can get that ready for you next Friday. The next load of women though, 'brides'" he laughed, "That'll take longer."

Pete was feeling full of himself, more than ready to step into

Jay's shoes. "Both, man, I'll take both. I'll have Vince and Tony run down there Friday night, and you can let me know when the women come in. And hey, I owe you."

"Of course you owe me. Be sure those fat muscle heads bring it with them when they come. I'm not running a fucking charity here."

Pete threw the phone on the table next to him and picked up the first slice of pizza. It was just cool enough not to blister and he savored each bite. Damn, he was in it now.

CHAPTER TWENTY-TWO

"Here, Mama, Here!" PJ was jumping up and down at the door as Carolyn came and scooped him up. Together they opened the door and watched Janine pull up in her small SUV. She could see her friend grinning and waving, her daughter April peering eagerly around a stack of laundry baskets. Once the car stopped, Carolyn and PJ hurried over to meet them. Janine hopped out and hugged both Carolyn and PJ at once. April was jumping in her booster seat and PJ was jumping in Carolyn's arms.

Janine opened the rear door and made quick work of the buckles holding April in place. Then she picked her up with a swift kiss on the cheek and set her down. Carolyn had set PJ down as well and the two were now jumping up and down together, happy to be reunited. Carolyn could see Rupert and Rusty waiting by the door so she took Carolyn by the elbow and ushered the children ahead of them to the door.

"Janine, this is Rupert Johns and his grandson, Rusty. Rupert, Rusty, this is my friend, Janine Stanford, and her daughter, April."

"From Baltimore?" Rusty asked. PJ had been talking nonstop about his friends' arrival and apparently Rusty had proven to be a good audience.

Janine laughed. "Well, like Carolyn I'm a military brat so I've lived all over. But you're right, April and I have been living in Baltimore." She shook hands with both men and stood gaping at the interior. "Carolyn, this is unreal! Look at this place! Do you pinch yourself when you wake up?"

Carolyn laughed and hugged her friend's shoulder. "Yep, most mornings!"

Rupert spoke up then, a broad smile on his face. "You two go on in and say hi to Helen. Rusty and I will take care of bringing in Ms. Stanford's things."

Janine stopped and turned, "Are you sure? I'm afraid it's a bit of a mess."

"No worries, Miss, Rusty and I are old hands at this. If you'll give me the keys we'll pull around near your quarters and take care of everything." Keys in hand he gestured to his grandson and they moved to take care of the luggage.

Once they had gone and Carolyn and Janine had stepped inside, Janine squeezed her friend's hand and giggled. "Our quarters? You have a freaking butler! I can't get over it all!"

Carolyn laughed at her friend and led the small group on into the house. "You're going to love it here, both of you. Let's go meet Rupert's wife, Helen. Then we'll go on a grand tour."

On their way to the kitchen they peeked into a few rooms, Janine gushing and shaking her head at their beauty. "This is unbelievable." PJ and April had run on ahead, following the tantalizing scent of fresh apple pie. Helen was just setting it out to cool when Carolyn and Janine walked in.

"Helen, that is gorgeous and it smells even better!" The pie had a deep brown crust with delicate pieces of pastry cut to look like apples, on one side.

Helen beamed. "We can enjoy it with our lunch. Hi, I'm Helen and this little charmer must be your April." PJ and April were already clambering up to the enormous kitchen island, fresh cups of milk awaiting them along with a bowl of animal crackers.

Janine reached out her hand, "What a welcome! That pie looks amazing, especially after two days of road food."

"Mama, can Apil play? Please?"

Helen stepped forward. "You two go take some time to yourselves, get Janine settled and I'll let everyone know when it's time for lunch."

Carolyn hesitated. "We're not trying to make more work for you."

"Work, are you kidding? Getting to chase these cuties around is nothing like work, believe me. And Janine, Rupert and I are happy to have you here!"

Carolyn and Janine stepped away from the kitchen then and moved toward another section of the house. Janine continued to ooh and ah as they walked, but at the library she was practically speechless. She ran her hand along a shelf of books and took a step up the tall brass ladder. "I've been using this as my office. When it's chilly Rupert even makes a fire for me." Carolyn gestured toward the fireplace and the chairs that sat in front of it. "I'm so glad you're here with me, it's really going to happen, we're going to open a school. Can you believe it?"

Janine dropped into the chair across from the desk and shook her head. "No, honestly, I can't wrap my head around any of yet, Carolyn. Seeing all of this, it's so much more than I imagined. I feel like I need to put on dress clothes or something and my God, I packed our things in laundry baskets. Your butler is unpacking a car filled with laundry baskets and kids' toys." She gestured at the space around them. "How have you gotten used to it all so fast?"

Carolyn sat down behind the desk and wondered the same thing. "I don't know really. It feels like Helen and Rupert just whisked us in and made us feel at home right away. I got busy with the school planning and then one thing just led to another. It is weird though."

Janine grinned. "Weird but awesome, girl! Let's see this school of yours." Janine hopped up and Carolyn led the way to the bright atrium classroom. She was so proud of the work she'd done but hesitant, wondering if Janine would see what she saw. In Baltimore and back at Penn State, Carolyn had worked in several different special education programs and the one constant factor was that the spaces were always hand-me-downs, programs set up in rooms that no one wanted. Here, finally, was something brand new. Carolyn held her breath as Janine walked in and twirled slowly around. Then she walked toward the yellow section where the small tables and easels were set up and waiting.

"I get to teach here? This is amazing!"

Carolyn let out her breath and laughed. "Oh, thank God, I was so afraid of what you'd say."

Janine turned toward her friend, " I love it, I love the rainbow and the big windows." She pointed toward the patio. "What's out there?"

Carolyn beamed. "It's our own tiny safety town, if you can believe it." Together they walked out onto the patio and stepped onto the small 'roads'. Over to the side, the bikes were parked under their own small lean to.

Janine laughed, "Wait until April sees this." She laughed. "Heck, I want to ride on it!" Just as she said that, a young squeal sounded behind them and PJ and April came at a run.

"Mama, Mama, can we ride?" Carolyn waved at Helen as she smiled and turned back toward her kitchen.

"Lunch will be ready in about half an hour, dear!" she called as she left.

PJ was tugging on Carolyn's hand now. "Bikes, Mama, bikes, peez?"

Carolyn laughed. "Of course. Let's show April and Janine how it works."

For the next half hour the children played happily on the trikes, careening back and forth, stopping suddenly when Rusty the 'policeman' showed up to direct them. Carolyn and Janine stepped back into the classroom and leaned against the teacher's desk that was in the center.

Janine rubbed her hands together. "I can't wait to get started."

"That is music to my ears because we have our first few students coming on Monday morning to join our two, and then the Open House is set for Thursday. My mom is staying here now so she can keep an eye on PJ and April while we're going over the details."

Janine paused, "so how's she doing?" In their communication Carolyn had not offered too much detail about Angela's condition. She shrugged her shoulders now as she attempted to explain.

"It's hard to say. She's still getting used to being here for one, and I think she does genuinely enjoy spending time with PJ. I guess you'd say it's kind of up and down. She has a good doctor. In fact you'll meet her daughter tomorrow. They're both Dr. Gilberts, Grace is mom's doctor and Susan is going to be our psychologist, working with me and a couple of people from the elementary on evaluations." Carolyn stood, unwilling to say much more about Angela. So far there hadn't been any more sundowning episodes and for that she was grateful. "You and April will be staying in the rooms that are at the end of this hallway." She glanced toward the patio before calling out to Rusty to bring everyone in to lunch soon.

Rusty waved. "Sure thing, Carolyn!" and returned to supervising the little tricyclists.

They walked on down the long hall until they came to a suite of rooms. The first door opened into a large seating area all decorated in blue and rose with a comfortable looking sofa, several arm chairs and a dark wooden rocker. Carolyn gestured toward a wooden cabinet that sat opposite the sofa. "There's a TV in there if you're interested and PJ picked out a few of his DVD's to share with April." Janine smiled but continued to stare in wonder as they moved through the space. A granite-topped bar separated the sitting area from an efficiency kitchen with its own two burner stove and refrigerator. Next, a short hallway led to three rooms. The first two were bedrooms, one had a broad queen sized bed covered in a homey, thick block quilt. A dark wooden dresser stood next to a deep closet. Janine walked all the way into the closet and shut the door before coming back out, laughing incredulously.

"Carolyn, this just isn't real!" They walked through a bathroom that held a deep tub, standing shower and double vanity. "Oh, Lord, you mean April and I will have to share?" She pretended to lean her head in despair as Carolyn joined in her laughter.

The two of them walked on into April's room, painted a cozy pink it held two twin beds and had a bay window with a seat built into it. They plopped on to the cushioned bench and looked around.

"This is so beautiful." She gestured around her. "April is going to love this room."

Carolyn grinned. "All right, here's the final test." The two walked back into the hallway and Carolyn opened up the last of the three doors. This room was larger than either of the bedrooms with a wall of windows and a door that opened onto a small, white patio. Rupert and Rusty had settled the baskets and boxes from Janine's car but they only took up a small space along one wall. Against the far wall there was a short counter with upper and lower cabinets around a wide sink. "I'm not sure what this space was designed for originally, Helen couldn't remember either. We just thought it might make a good studio area with the high ceiling and all the natural light from the windows." Carolyn waited, unsure what Janine's reaction would be. Her friend had walked over to the windows and the pause grew.

When Janine finally turned around, Carolyn was shocked to see she was crying. Janine pulled a crumpled tissue from her pocket and dabbed at her eyes, her tears slowly replaced with a smile. Then she pulled her friend into a fierce hug. "I'm never leaving!"

Carolyn laughed then and hung onto her friend. "Oh thank God, you scared me. I was so afraid it wasn't right."

Janine hesitated a moment before going on. "I packed up all of my canvases and supplies but I told Sean not to send them until I checked the place out. Now," she grinned at Carolyn, "I can't wait for it all to get here!"

After another brief hug, they made their way back toward the center of the house and the kitchen area. Janine laughed, "I feel like I'm going to need to leave a trail of breadcrumbs for a while, just to find my way!"

True to her word, Helen had lunch set up within the hour. Carolyn was a little shocked to see the places set at one end of the large, formal dining room. They only took up a section of the massive table and Helen had used simple placemats to make it seem a bit homier, but Carolyn was still taken aback. She looked at Helen, chagrined, as the children, her mother and Janine all sat down with Helen, Rupert and Rusty. "I guess we were getting a bit big for the other table." She worried about the extra work that was already piling onto Helen and Rupert's shoulders and Carolyn took a moment to pull Helen aside as the others were sitting down. "Are you sure that you and Rupert are okay with all of this?" Carolyn gestured at the group, watching Helen's face for a response. She hoped she would be able tell a forced one from a genuine.

Carolyn was surprised when Helen pulled her into a warm hug. "Honey, you have no idea how lonely the three of us were, even when Mr. Clark was still here. This was a grand place at one time and his wife filled it with friends and family. But once she passed, it was just the four of us rattling around in this monstrosity." She gestured toward the group, a wide grin settling on her features.

"Don't you see, there's life again and you're letting us be a part of all of that."

Carolyn took a moment to hug Helen back. "If you're sure, but we have to hire on some more help, for kitchen prep and cleaning at the very least."

Helen nodded as they moved toward the table. "You won't catch me arguing with you about that! A friend of mine's granddaughter has been looking for work. I think I'll give her a call this afternoon if that's all right with you."

"That sounds perfect Helen." Carolyn smiled as she joined the bubbling group at the table. They started to pass plates back and forth when a giggle arose from Janine. "I feel like I just fell through the looking glass into the weirdest summer camp ever!" Carolyn was pleased that everyone, even her mother, was laughing.

CHAPTER TWENTY-THREE

*W*hile Janine and April went off to get settled into their new space, Carolyn led PJ back to their rooms for a nap. She hadn't told him yet that his dad was coming that afternoon. She figured he'd never fall asleep once he knew, so she settled him in with a few stories and then closed the door quietly behind her. She noticed that her mother wasn't in her bedroom and was relieved when she spotted her in their little sitting area, by the window. Reading or dozing she couldn't be sure but either way, Angela looked contented and for that, Carolyn was thankful. She carried the baby monitor back with her into the library and settled down to work.

When Carolyn heard PJ stirring, she was shocked to see that an hour and a half had just whizzed by. She got up from her computer and went to meet him. He was pretty good about staying in his bed, but Carolyn didn't want him to wonder where she was. "Hey, little buddy." She scooped him up and carried him into the bathroom. "I have a surprise."

"More than Apil?" he asked as he stretched to reach the big toilet. He took care of business and stood on his step stool to wash his hands.

Carolyn handed him the towel and then held his hand as he hopped down. "Yep. Your daddy is coming to see you this afternoon. He wants to take you to see his new apartment." PJ looked puzzled.

"What's apartment?" he asked.

"An apartment is a kind of small house, your daddy has a room just for you."

PJ still looked puzzled. "Can Apil come, too?"

Carolyn shook her head. "No, I'm afraid not, buddy, but she'll be here when you get back. Let's find some clothes for you to wear, maybe something a little bit warmer." Carolyn was able to talk him into a long sleeved shirt and some soft pants. He was still fairly new to potty training and the easier the pants were to get off, the better chance he'd have. He wasn't thrilled when she insisted that he wear shoes, but he picked out the ones that lit up when he ran so he was placated if not exactly happy. Carolyn took a moment to look in her mirror and was mildly disappointed at what she saw. She took a few minutes to put on a more flattering top and ran a brush through her long hair. There wasn't time for make-up but she did switch from her worn out old clogs into a pair of short boots that the salesman had insisted were stylish. Carolyn had never had any interest in fashion so she'd just had to take his word.

While she finished getting ready, PJ rushed to the kitchen to tell Helen where he was going.

"See Daddy apartment." he nodded at Helen as she handed him a banana from the wide fruit bowl.

"Well, you're going to need some energy for that adventure," she advised and helped him to tear the peel down. "Oh, don't you look nice, dear!" When she walked in, Helen beamed at Carolyn who blushed, already feeling silly that she'd changed clothes for what would most likely be a three-minute encounter.

Helen smiled and thankfully changed the subject. "My friend's granddaughter is coming over in the morning so we can size her up. She's taking a gap year right now, trying to decide which direction she wants to go in so I think she'll be just perfect." The doorbell rang and Helen could see Carolyn tense. She whispered, "You can do this, dear," then gave her a gentle push toward the door. Rupert was heading for it as well but Helen waved him off and Carolyn went forward, her chin high and her knees wobbling slightly.

Carolyn opened the door wide and PJ came running. Alex bent and scooped him up in a hug.

"Hey, little man. How're you doing?"

"Partment," PJ nodded to his dad. Alex smiled and nodded back, then set him down and turned to Carolyn.

"Hi, Carolyn." He leaned forward and placed a small kiss on her cheek. Carolyn tried not to make too much of it, but was glad that she'd taken a moment to change.

"Come in." She smiled. "I just have a few notes for you." Carolyn handed him a sheet of notebook paper that was more than half filled with instructions. "He's still pretty new to potty training so I wanted to let you know what he's used to.

"Daddy has potty?" PJ looked up and Alex bent down to his level.

"You bet I do, it's probably just like yours." He smiled at PJ and looked over the note.

Carolyn held her breath. In addition to the bathroom instructions she had made a long list of emergency numbers including poison control. She was afraid he would make fun of her for it, but he tucked it into his pocket and grinned.

"You look great, Caro," He gestured at the big house around them. "I have to say, this job sure seems to agree with you. I'd like to hear more about it when you have the time."

Carolyn smiled and nodded but didn't offer up any specifics. "Do you know when you'll have him back?"

"Would eight be too late?"

Carolyn hesitated for just a moment but then let it go. Normally, PJ'd be in bed before that but she figured the novelty of it all would carry him through. "Sure, that sounds fine." She opened the door and stood aside as Alex picked PJ up once more. "Do you have a..."

"Car seat?' he finished. "Yep, installed it yesterday." He rested his hand on Carolyn's arm. "I'll take good care of him, Caro, I swear."

Carolyn looked at him, seeing the new lines that edged the familiar blue eyes. She reached over and kissed PJ on the top of his head. "I know you will. Be good now, PJ, see you later!"

"Bye mama, later alligator!" he giggled and Alex moved away. Carolyn watched as Alex buckled him into the car seat, closed the rear door and climbed in behind the wheel. He gave her a quick wave and was gone.

"Was that Alex?" Carolyn jumped, unaware that Janine had walked up behind her.

Carolyn felt so strange she wasn't sure what to say. She felt sad and halfway guilty letting PJ go but she also felt a little bit embarrassed by her reaction to seeing Alex. Something still stirred inside her at his touch. She nodded at her friend but didn't offer any comment, especially once she realized Janine was probably able to read every thought as it made its way across her features.

She gave Carolyn's shoulder a squeeze. "He looks good and PJ looked thrilled. Let's go do some work!"

Carolyn grinned at her friend and linked her arm in hers. "You got it. How do you feel about spreadsheets and party planning?"

Janine laughed. "Oh joy, lead on!" The two friends returned to the library and worked on school details until time for supper.

When she heard the car return with PJ and Alex, Carolyn was sitting at the small table with Angela having a cup of tea. As Carolyn went to usher them in, Angela rose and carried her cup to the sink. "Good night, dear," she called and whisked out of the room before Carolyn could speak. When she got the door open,

Alex reached around the sleeping boy and quickly put his finger to his lips. "He's out cold," he whispered. Carolyn smiled and gestured for him to come in. "He went to the bathroom right before we got in the car so I think he'll be okay for the night." Carolyn nodded and gestured for Alex to follow her to PJ's bedroom. He laid him down gently, pulled off his shoes and then spread the blankets over him. Carolyn touched her fingers to her lips and then rested them on PJ's forehead for a second.

"Sleep tight, little one," she whispered. She picked up the monitor and carried it with her back out to the kitchen. "Can I get you some tea?" she asked, then motioned for Alex to take the chair that Angela had been using.

"No, thanks, I'm good."

Carolyn sat down across from him and tucked her hands just under her thighs in an effort to steady her nerves. "So, how'd it go?"

He spread his hands out wide on his knees and leaned back in the seat. "It was great. Well," he shrugged, "a little bit rocky at first actually. My upstairs neighbor has a big dog and he started barking right as we were walking in. But, once we got past those tears, I think it went all right. He seemed to like the room I'd fixed up for him but he wasn't quite sure about a sleep over." Alex looked up, as though he were searching Carolyn's face for clues. "I think you're right that he isn't ready for that yet. I'm okay taking it slow."

"Really?" Carolyn couldn't explain why she felt so relieved. A tiny part of her must have been afraid that Alex would quickly woo her little boy away from her somehow. She picked up her teacup and was pleased to see that her hands appeared steady. "How's the new job?"

Alex rubbed his hand across his eyes briefly and then looked up. "It's good, I think. These recruits, though, they're so young, they're babies. They're eager, I'll give them that, but so green. Not all of them will make it through the training, that's for sure."

"But you like the work?"

"Sure," Alex nodded. "The nine-to-five bit is a little weird, but I'm getting used to it."

Carolyn sensed that there might be more of a struggle there than he was admitting. "Not very thrilling, I imagine?"

He paused and then took his time in answering. "I realize now what a thrill junky I've been. The academy addresses some of that in its classes, downplaying the excitement, coaching the recruits about the power of adrenaline." He shrugged, "To be honest, some days I feel just fine with the new routine, especially when I think about what happened to Chris and Juan. But other days," he rubbed his hands along his jeans. "Sometimes I feel more like an addict in need of a twelve-step program than I do an instructor." He looked again at Carolyn and took a deep breath but didn't say any more. He got up to leave and Carolyn followed him to the door. "I've got a half day off on Thursday, could I come by for him around 12:30? I figure, put him down for a nap at my place, let him get a little more used to it."

Carolyn smiled. "That would be awesome, actually. Our open house is Thursday and I'll probably be crazy busy that afternoon. If you brought him home at six we could have a quick dinner and you could see the program."

Alex gestured around him. "That'd be terrific. My curiosity is definitely piqued when it comes to this place. I'll see you then!" He looked as though maybe he wanted to reach for her, to kiss her before he had to go, but he settled for a quick wave instead.

Carolyn closed and locked the door behind her, awash in a variety of emotions, not all of which she could name. She shook her head back and forth wondering what to make of it all, of Alex, of the house and school, even the court case. Never had so much been riding on her shoulders. She washed her teacup and Angela's and returned them to the cupboard. She flipped off the last of the light switches and made her way through the house, marveling again at the sheer size of a place that could swallow up so many different people and lives and yet remain so quiet.

CHAPTER TWENTY-FOUR

By Monday morning Pete was feeling jazzed, getting back into the game, he told himself. Now he just needed to get his hands on some cash so that he'd be ready for Friday's shipment. Jay's condo was in a new development on the east side of the city, a penthouse suite on top of a nondescript block of steel and aluminum. Pete knew Jay loved that shit but he couldn't stand it. Give him an old house in a real neighborhood any day. He drove around the block twice, identifying the two police cars that were set up around the place. He noticed that both pairs of cops looked either bored or sleepy and he figured the detail had been running too long to remain efficient. When a car with an Uber sticker on it entered the parking lot, Pete followed in closely before turning left into a low traffic corner of the lot. He watched out his windows for a few minutes, checking to see what the cops would do. He saw one fat, older guy go up to the Uber driver and ask him questions, but no one else seemed to be moving. Once he spotted a tenant exiting a side door and heading for the ride, he walked over and slipped inside.

Pete wasn't heading for the penthouse. So he figured even if one of the lazy assed cops followed him, they wouldn't care. Instead, he was heading down the back stairs to the lowest level where a utility closet sat next to a huge tenant storage area. Jay had taken him down there once before and he'd been surprised then by the size of it. Why did people accumulate so much shit, he wondered? He worked his way past wire cages that seemed to hold everything from extra furniture to doghouses. In the middle was Jay's. He recognized the plain, unlabeled boxes and the distinct lack of clutter. He pulled the slim pick from his jacket pocket and was quickly through the lock and inside the unit. He could see where the boxes had been opened, probably by the cops. Folded clothes were visible in one of them, tattered books in the second. Pete figured they were both fakes. He moved directly to the box that was pressed farthest back against the wall partly opened and filled with discarded winter coats. Bits of down floated just above the box as he shifted it aside. He lifted it carefully and reached underneath where a stack of bills was taped to the underside. It wasn't a fortune by any means, just a hundred thousand or so, but it would be enough for Friday, he figured. He stashed the money in the back of his pants beside his revolver, then pulled his jacket down over both. He paused and listened carefully, but heard nothing.

Pete made his way back up to the side door and looked out the window, studying the cops' whereabouts before moving forward. One was at the door of the other police car with his back to Pete and shielding the view of the other cop, shooting the shit. Pete slipped easily out to his car and tucked the cash into a pouch he had sewn underneath the driver's seat. Then he spotted a second exit to the lot near a loading dock and took off to make a second stop. He knew of a pawnshop near downtown where the owner was into photography. He had the agent's laptop with him and aimed to make a bit more money, this time for himself. A bell jangled over the door as he walked in. "Hey man, what's up?" Pete tried for a friendly tone.

The owner, an older guy nodded briefly and moved forward to the counter. "What can I do for you?"

"So, uh, I heard you're into photography, that right?"

"Gray Sokolov," he extended his hand over the counter. "Yes, I am, you?"

"Phil Smith, ah yeah, I've been taking pictures for a while now." He brought the laptop up and set it on the scratched glass countertop. "You ever buy any photographs or know someone else who does?" Pete tried for an affable type of grin. "I'm thinking about getting into the business."

The owner nodded, "Yeah, I know a few. What've you got?" He gestured toward the laptop and Pete opened it eagerly. He'd pulled one file up, ready to page through the images when he saw a look flicker across the man's face. "What's wrong?"

He knew the pawnshop owner must be used to dealing with rough characters, but the sight of the agent's photograph on the screen seemed to have taken him by surprise. "Nothing," he blustered, "just thought that background photo looked familiar for a minute."

Pete studied his face for a moment longer. "You did, huh?" He paused, waiting to see if there'd be more of a reaction. "So, how much you think they're worth?"

"Uh, I'd buy the whole laptop off you if you're selling," he offered. He tried to look the man in the eye but was struggling to hold his composure.

Pete slapped the laptop closed and tucked it back under his arm. "Wasn't trying to sell the laptop, now was I?" He reached behind him for his gun and pulled it out rapidly, waving the man out from behind the counter with it.

Gray raised his hands in the air, frustrated that he hadn't had time to push his alarm button or grab the gun he kept under the cash drawer. "Dude, you don't want to sell, that's fine with me." He was a tall, thin man, with the build of a runner not a fighter. "Listen, I don't want any trouble here."

Pete grinned, "I don't want any trouble either." He shot the man in his left knee, then turned to leave. "See that there isn't any."

Pete left quickly, the laptop still in his hands and dashed for his car. Fuck, that was a stupid move. He had no idea what the man knew, why he'd looked that way at the laptop but he couldn't take any chances. Probably should have shot him in the head he thought, as he climbed in his car and headed home.

Back in the shop, Gray moaned with the pain in his knee and tried to bend forward. He wanted to put something on it to stop the bleeding but he couldn't. He spotted his jacket looped over a chair near the counter and managed to pull it and the chair down without knocking himself out. He reached inside for his cell phone and dialed 911.

"911. What's your emergency?"

"Aaah," he moaned again. "I've been shot in the knee. Help, please!" Gray passed out then before he could hear the operator's response. When he came to, a young EMT was leaning over him attaching a blood pressure cuff to his arm. Someone else seemed to be wrapping something around his knee and he yelled out with the pain.

"We've got you sir, it's going to be all right" the man with the cuff addressed him and gestured toward his partner. "She's just putting a wrap around your knee to stop the bleeding. We'll have you at the hospital in no time."

While the EMT patted Gray on the shoulder, he felt himself go under again. God, it hurt so much.

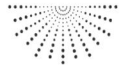

CHAPTER TWENTY-FIVE

The next day, Ray and Cindy were heading back to the car after getting lunch when Cindy's phone rang.

The caller ID read hospital. "Hello?"

"Is this Cindy O'Brien?"

"Yes, may I help you?'

"Ma'am, I'm calling from UPMC Mercy Hospital and we have a man in our ER who asked me to call you. His name is Gray Sokolov. He's been shot."

"Shot? I'll be right there." She hung up before the person could say any more. She and Ray were racing toward the car. "Which hospital?" he asked.

"Mercy, the ER." They buckled in quickly and Ray pulled out the little used emergency light and affixed it to the roof.

Within minutes, they were pulling up to the ER lot. Cindy jumped out while Ray parked. She was still waiting at the guest desk when he got inside.

"Gray Sokolov, I received a call from here just a few minutes ago." She flipped open her ID and waited while the young woman pulled up the information.

"I'm sorry, our system has been super slow today. Here he is, room 4, straight back and to your left, through the double doors. Cindy nodded her thanks and the two of them slapped visitor stickers on their chests as they moved forward.

"So who is Gray Sokolov?" Ray asked as they reached the double doors."

"He's my friend the photographer, the one with the pawnshop." They passed through the doors with a swoosh and searched for room number 4. When they reached it, Ray held back a step and let Cindy go in ahead of him. The man in the bed looked as gray as his name. His left leg was wrapped in layers of bloody gauze and hung from a sling above the bed. An IV poked out of his left arm so Cindy reached over gingerly to give him a peck on the cheek. "What happened, Gray? They told me you were shot."

A wide grin spread across his face, then morphed into a wince as he struggled to sit taller. "Thank God you're okay. I was so afraid something had happened to you."

"What do you mean? What happened?" She sat down gingerly on the side of the bed and held the older man's thin hand in hers.

"I was in my shop this afternoon and this man came in with a laptop. He said he was a photographer and he asked me if I wanted to buy some pictures. When he opened up the laptop, the screen was your shot of the skyline. I tried to play it cool, act like I didn't know anything, but I must have given something away just with the look on my face. When he pulled out the gun, I was sure I was a dead man but I was even more afraid that you were dead already." He grasped her hand tightly.

Ray entered the room them and stepped quietly beside Cindy. "Gray, this is Ray, the, uh, the man I told you about."

A wide grin spread across his face, and he turned to Cindy, "the agent?"

Cindy couldn't help but blush. "Ray Sanchez, Gray Sokolov."

Ray nodded but didn't try to take the man's hand from Cindy. "Good to meet you Gray, except" he raised his hand to gesture at the area around them, "for the circumstances. Can you tell us what the man looked like?"

"Uh sure, not too tall, mid-50s maybe, salt and pepper hair, kind of on the long side." He gestured at his neckline. I described him to the police earlier." Ray spotted the copy of a police report on the bedside table.

"May I?" Ray took the paper and stepped out into the hall.

"Sure," Gray nodded but then lowered his head back in pain. A nurse entered then and Cindy stepped out into the hallway with Ray. "What do you think?"

Ray handed her the police report to read while he dialed his phone. "I'm going to ask the detective to send over photos for your friend to look through, a stack with Pete Turner in it." His call connected and he stepped back out into the larger hallway. The nurse re-opened the door and allowed Cindy back in.

Gray was looking a little more crestfallen when Cindy came up to the bed. She took his hand again. "The nurse said they're going to give me the anesthetic soon and take me to surgery."

"Is there someone I can call for you?"

Gray gestured to the small table where his jacket and a set of keys were resting. "My cell's in the pocket of my jacket. Could you call my sister? She's on the speed dial at the top."

"Sure thing," Cindy smiled and located the phone. She confirmed his sister's number with Gray and then stepped back out into the hall to call.

Ray returned then, an eager look on his face.

"The detective sent me a file with a bunch of photos."

"Well we'd better hurry, they're about to start prepping him for surgery." They walked into the room together and Cindy tucked Gray's phone back into his jacket. "Your sister's on her way Gray." He looked relieved.

Ray stepped up to the bedside then. "Gray, could you look at a few pictures, see if you recognize the man who shot you?" Gray tried to sit up but Ray waved him back and brought his phone over where the man could see the photos. "I'll just page through them slowly, you tell me if I need to stop."

Ray showed the various photographs, silently counting out an even beat to be sure that he wasn't pushing one photo over another. As soon as the fifth one appeared, the man's hand shot out, his finger pointing directly at Pete Turner. "That's the guy. His hair's a little longer but that's him." He looked up at both Ray and Cindy.

Ray closed his phone just as a new nurse arrived with the anesthetist. "You did great, Gray. Now let's let them help you." Cindy reached over and gave Gray one more kiss on the cheek.

"I'll check back in the morning. Just rest and get better, okay?"

"I'll do my best," he smiled and squeezed Cindy's hand for a second before the hospital staff got to work and she and Ray drove back to the office.

Although they now had clear confirmation that Turner was the one who had been in Cindy's apartment, there wasn't much else that they could do for the moment. Ray had conveyed Gray's identification to the police officer in charge but they'd had to leave it at that. Once at the office, the two parted ways heading for their separate desks.

Cindy was able to locate the state park from the photograph, a place called Hammock's Beach. On a map, the park appeared to be made up of a mainland section and an undeveloped barrier island. It boasted campsites and a snack bar but little else. There was a ferry service that ran between the coast and island but this time of year it's service was limited to weekends only. She called down there but it went to an automated answering system. She left her home and cell number as well as the office one but wasn't particularly confident that she would hear from them. "Okay, Arnie," she said to herself. "Let's take a look back at your financial records, see if we can't find some connection."

Downstairs Ray had just sat down at his desk when a roar

seemed to come from the glassed in office at the end of the wide room. "Son of a bitch!" His captain could be heard shouting. Other agents joined Ray as they stood and came to the outer door.

"What's up, chief?" another agent called out.

"That fucking, spineless DA has dropped almost all of the charges against Jay Warren." He kicked the side of the nearest file cabinet as he slammed his fist into his palm. "Attempted manslaughter against the Rogers woman."

Ray stepped up, "you shitting me? With all the dirt we've got on that family? What about the plane crash? He killed his father for God's sake!"

"Shit," the captain sat down heavily on the nearest desk, "of course we know all that, the DA's saying we can't prove it. He says that since there're witnesses from the shooting at the restaurant, that's the best we can do."

Angry conversations swirled, as Ray stood dumbfounded in the center. "What's the most he could get? 5 to 10?"

"You got that right. I'm going back at him, see if I can't shake something else loose. You've got less than two weeks to find me more or this asshole is going to get away with murder and be back on our streets."

The agents in the room broke up into groups of two and three. Ray left them and bounded up the stairs to Cindy's desk. By the stunned look on her face, he could see that the news had already reached her. He threw himself into her extra chair, his head in his hands. "What the hell, Ray, attempted manslaughter, that's it? How can that be?"

Ray leaned back in the seat and spread his hands out wide on his knees. "It just feels like giving up to me, like somebody above our pay grade has just given up."

"Or been bought," she posited.

He tilted his head. "Bought, you think so?"

"Ray, we have no idea just how far this family's reach extends. They may have all kinds of people in their pockets."

"Well, I'm not giving up that easy. D'you find anything yet?"

"Maybe. Take a look at this." She went through the information about the park, before turning to show him a spreadsheet. "I found this account under his name, not his wife's. All of the other accounts that we went through in the spring were joint. But this one seems to have been used for business. There are bills from Lulu's, regular cash deposits from sources that I can't locate and what look like other business expenses to office supply stores and such. But this, this is what caught my eye just now."

"It's a rental car. That doesn't seem that unusual."

Cindy nodded. "You're right, but look, it's not for here in the city. It's from Richmond, Virginia. There's a hotel bill from the same week."

"So you think he went out of town on business? That still doesn't seem that unusual to me."

Cindy grinned, "Look way down here. It's a charge for gas in a small town in North Carolina called Jacksonville. I looked it up. It's the last town of any size that you would go through on your way to this state park."

"Wow." Ray's face lit up. "When was it?"

Cindy sank back in her chair. "Nearly a year ago, I'm afraid."

But Ray's expression remained eager, "that's all right, the big court case was already swirling around back then. He could have decided to get out once that began roiling around the city. Maybe he was afraid he'd be arrested along with the bigger players. At least it's a place to start."

Cindy nodded, "you're right. Let's take a look at Hanes's financials and see if we can link them together on any of the information." Cindy split the computer screen between the list of charges on Arnie Lowe's account and the charges they'd found on

Greg Hanes's bank and credit card records. She was paging down when Ray's hand darted out.

"There, there's a Lulu's charge for both of them on the same night."

Cindy highlighted them and then three more that they found. "Let's see what Hanes was doing while Arnie was in North Carolina."

They looked through the charges twice but could find no connection. "Damn, looks like Hanes was still here in the city, so it wasn't a rendezvous." Just then an additional page began to load from Greg Hanes's account.

Cindy nearly jumped in her seat. There was a $25 charge to the Urgent Care place they'd already located but beneath the one she'd seen before from Richmond, there was now an additional transaction. "He emptied the account."

"How, online somewhere? Could we trace it?"

Cindy shook her head, a broad grin spreading across her face. "It was done in person," she pointed at the entry on the screen. "Jacksonville, North Carolina"

Ray leapt to his feet. "We've got him, he's got to be there."

"Wait, wait," Cindy turned her chair away from the computer so that she could face where he was pacing back and forth. "What are you thinking?"

Ray threw himself back into the chair but leaned forward eagerly. "What if that's where Hanes is hiding? You said it's a small park, right, we could go talk to him there."

"But the bureau will never approve this kind of wild goose chase, we don't have anything more than a hunch. They'll never pay to fly us down there, you know that, especially if they've already agreed to scale back the charges. We ask, they'll probably tell us to shelve the whole case, move on."

Ray took off his glasses and rubbed his eyes before looking up at Cindy. ""I think we should give it a couple of days, see if the cops can get Pete Turner under wraps." He grinned, "then, I'm thinking 'road trip'!"

She thought of the tedium she'd spent the morning wading through on her computer, and grinned back at him. "I'm in if you are, as long as I can take my camera," she paused, "and use my car."

"Your car? What do you mean?"

"I'm not interested in taking a road trip in that POS junker that you call a car. There's a reason you drive an agency car whenever you can."

"Hey it's vintage." He couldn't help but grin.

Cindy shrugged. "One man's vintage is another man's POS! I have a fondness for windows that close all the way and a stereo system that works out of more than one speaker at a time!"

He reached his hand out to her but then ducked in for a quick kiss. "You win. Let's pick up some dinner Thursday evening and take off that night. He grinned at her as she nodded and then headed downstairs to work on clearing off his desk.

CHAPTER TWENTY-SIX

*T*he morning was cool but bright and the sunshine streaming in the big windows was an energizing site, as Janine and Carolyn welcomed their first students. There was a pair of twins from over in the next development and a very small, quiet, boy named Davey who belonged to the board member she'd met during the street negotiations. PJ and April were present as part of the welcoming committee and quickly ushered the other children into the classroom The two sets of parents waited and watched for a while as Carolyn settled the children in the blue classroom area and began the program. Later, she took a moment to confer with Janine. "How did the parents seem as they were leaving?"

Janine smiled. "Good, really good. I think they all expected tears but with April and PJ leading the way the kids got engaged quickly. I was impressed and I think they were too."

The morning continued to go well and both Carolyn and Janine were surprised when twelve o'clock arrived and the parents reappeared at the door. The twins ran over to their mother quickly and were excitedly telling her about April and the school. Davey walked quietly over to his mother and smiled but didn't offer any comments. The parents and children all left and PJ and April ran off toward the kitchen. Carolyn and Janine took a few moments to meet up in the center of the room.

Carolyn exhaled. "We did it! One day down, hundreds more to go! What'd you think?"

Janine plopped down on one of the small chairs and smiled up at her friend. "I think you have a hit, my friend. It was a good start. I still can't believe there weren't any tears, from the kids or the parents."

After lunch, Janine volunteered to settle PJ and April down with stories and naps while Carolyn met with Susan to review their evaluation plan. The young student arrived at 1:00 P.M. with her mother and the group worked together for about two hours. The evaluation began well and both Carolyn and Susan were pleased with their arrangements. The testing room had been small enough for the little girl to get comfortable and Carolyn had been able to interview her mother in the office area next door. When they finished, everyone had been given a tour of the classroom and both mother and child appeared eager to continue the process. They would meet again on Tuesday afternoon to continue the evaluation with the elementary school's speech pathologist and Wednesday morning, Annie would join their morning playgroup. Both Carolyn and Susan assured the mother that Annie's evaluation would continue as she participated in the program and that they would all sit down on Friday afternoon to make further plans.

Thursday's Open House arrived more quickly than Carolyn imagined. Both she and Janine were happy that the morning sessions had been going well. The weather all week had been unseasonably warm and the children had especially enjoyed their time outside on the trikes and bikes. Rusty had proven to be a wonderful 'traffic cop' and the children had loved stopping and starting, even crashing from time to time, under his careful eye.

Most surprising of all to Carolyn, was the interest that Angela had been showing in the program. On Monday and Tuesday she spent time watching through the one-way mirror. She had a few questions for Carolyn and Janine at lunch those days but she offered little comment. Wednesday morning, though, before the children arrived, Curt had appeared at the classroom door with her mother's old rocker in his hands. Carolyn stared speechless as Angela walked over and directed him to place it in a corner of the reading area.

Curt took off with a wave and Carolyn watched as Angela took a seat, adjusted the rocker's placement a bit and then looked up. "Mom?"

She had a broad smile on her face that Carolyn couldn't remember seeing in a long time. "Well, it just seemed like you needed a place for adults to sit, maybe to read a few stories from time to time."

Carolyn smiled back. "Would you like to do that Mom, have a regular story time with the children?"

"I'd like that," she answered and pivoted in the seat to look through some of the books.

"Well, all right then!" Carolyn grinned over at Janine who was standing in her art area, a look of wonder on her face. At mid-morning all of the children sat quietly, looking up at Angela as she read them three stories, each with animation and excitement. The transformation was startling and Carolyn couldn't resist sending her doctor an email describing Angela's participation.

On Thursday afternoon, while April napped and PJ visited with his dad, Janine and Carolyn got to work setting up their signs and decorations for the Open House. The party planner had done wonders for them and now Helen and her new assistant were busy preparing trays of snacks and fruit as well as small goody bags for any children who came along to see the program. At the elementary, the speech pathologist had been happy to hang up fliers for them and Carolyn knew of at least two families planning to come.

At five, Carolyn and Janine stood in the center of the classroom and looked around. "Well, I think we're as ready as we'll ever be!" Janine gave her a high five.

"We are set. I'll show people around and answer any general questions while you talk with the parents who want to enroll."

"You mean 'if' there are parents who want to enroll."

"Are you really that nervous Carolyn?" Janine looked quizzically. "You've got something amazing here, don't you know that? You built it and they will come," she chanted.

Carolyn grabbed her friend in a bear hug. "I'm so glad you're here! Have I told you that already?"

Janine laughed. "Just about every day but I can live with that!" The two laughed.

"All right, let's go get changed and get some dinner. Alex and PJ should be back soon."

By six the entire group was gathered at the dining table but there was so much excitement in the air, it wasn't clear if anyone was eating much. The Open House was due to run from seven to eight-thirty and PJ and April were going to be allowed in for a little while at the beginning.

Just before seven, Carolyn introduced Charlie Wright to Grace Gilbert and ushered both of them through the small tour. Alex accompanied them and she wondered what impressions he might be forming but other guests began to arrive and her attention was diverted. At seven-thirty he led the kids back in to Angela.

There was a good turnout but as eight twenty-five arrived, the crowd had thinned and only one set of parents was walking with Janine through the observation and testing area while Carolyn chatted with Charlie. Suddenly Rupert appeared at the inner classroom door.

"Miss, this gentleman arrived at the front door," she could hear the disapproval in his voice as the burly man pushed his way into the room, leaving a stunning young woman trailing behind.

Carolyn nodded at Rupert as she stepped forward and offered her hand, but she noticed that Rupert remained positioned by the door.

"Good evening, I'm Carolyn Jacobs and you are?" The man stood and surveyed the classroom but didn't answer and didn't take her hand. Carolyn turned to the young woman then and offered her hand again. The woman looked distracted but shook Carolyn's hand briefly before standing back and allowing the man to move forward. He walked slowly into the room and turned to look at the windows and the lighted patio.

Carolyn tried the young woman again. "Uh, are you looking for a preschool program for your child?"

The young woman snorted, "Oh, hell no, I mean, uh, no. Not at this time." The woman walked back to stand near Rupert in the doorway where they'd entered and Carolyn caught sight of Charlie waving to get her attention. He was mouthing something but she couldn't be sure what.

"I bet this was a goddamned beautiful room before you fucked it up this way." Carolyn stepped back toward her desk, appalled. Then she caught sight of the note Charlie had written on one of the brochures that was sitting there. 'James Warren' it said. Carolyn nearly choked. She was about to answer when Janine returned to the classroom area with the parents. The father was tall, and muscular but still, she feared for their safety. She picked up one of the other brochures and walked over to greet them, positioning herself between them and the man. She talked with them for a few minutes before ushering them out.

Then she turned to confront the man, drawing herself up to her full height. "What can I do for you, Mr. Warren?" She saw Janine blanch and move toward Charlie. Neither of them spoke.

"Just taking a look at my new property, that's all." He made a sound that might have been a laugh but held a more threatening tone to it.

"This is not your property, and it never will be," Carolyn spoke carefully. He looked at her, a leer spreading across his wide, slack face.

"We'll see about that." He jerked his hand toward the young woman. "C'mon, I've seen enough." He paused next to Rupert before bulldozing his way through the doorway. Rupert followed quickly behind them making sure that the man didn't make any detours.

Minutes later, Rupert and Helen arrived back in the classroom. Carolyn walked forward quickly. "Are you all right?" she asked Rupert.

He reached over and gave her a quick, unexpected hug. "I'm fine, Miss, we all are. I knew when he showed up that he was trouble, but I wasn't sure what could be done. I'm relieved that he left as easily as he did."

"You and me both." Carolyn nodded.

Charlie looked shaken and Carolyn pulled out the desk chair for him to sit down. He took a handkerchief from his pocket and wiped it across his brow. "I had no idea that onerous man would ever show up here. I'm so sorry."

"Sorry? You didn't do anything wrong, Charlie." By this time her fear had turned to anger. "What kind of person does that, shows up making threats?" Charlie started to answer but he saw her deflate just a bit. "I know, a Warren, that's who. Do we need to call the police, Charlie?"

He shook his head. "I don't think we can. We had a function that was open to the public and he came."

"To the *front door*," Rupert added.

Charlie nodded, "I know, it wasn't proper protocol." He gestured toward the outer door.

"We had clear signs all around the property directing people to this entrance Charlie," Janine added.

He nodded but didn't say anymore.

Carolyn began closing and locking the doors, shutting out the lights. "Let's go have a glass of wine. I don't think there's anything more we can do tonight and I don't want to think about the Warrens any more. Let's just celebrate how well the Open House went. We enrolled two more general education students and collected three referrals for special needs kids. I think that's a win in anyone's book."

"I'll second that," Janine added and followed Carolyn and the group back into the house.

CHAPTER TWENTY-SEVEN

*T*he last weekend that the ferry service was running, Greg was sitting behind the counter when he nodded off and somehow managed to fall off the chair. He was sleepy enough that it hadn't hurt much but he took a moment before rising to pull himself together. That's when he saw it. Under the counter, back against the outer wall, a small Ziploc bag taped just under the wooden lip. Greg shifted onto his hands and knees and crawled under far enough to pull it down. The tape was frayed and dried out from the heat but the baggie was still intact. Inside was a little figurine designed to look like a Lego spaceman, but when he pulled on it gently, the head came off to reveal a USB connector. Greg pocketed the drive and tore apart the wrapping before burying it in the garbage can. A wave equal parts joy and fear swept over him. It was like finding the brown park sign, as if Arnie was still moving him forward. He'd never told him anything about a hidden drive or a secret plan, but somehow, Greg knew this was Arnie's. Like Bill Nye, Arnie had always wanted to be an astronaut. But more importantly, he'd said the information he had on the Warrens was nowhere near his home or family. Leverage, not money, was the key to bringing down the Warrens. Greg prayed to God that was what he had in his pocket.

Later that night, once the campground had gone quiet, he settled on the concrete floor of the concession stand. The nights were starting to get a little cooler so he pulled on an old hooded sweatshirt as he waited for the unit to boot up. An animal outside the wall was scrabbling in the sand as the wind shifted in the trees above his head. Once the computer was up, he checked that he was completely off line before inserting the small drive. It began to load and he held his breath as page after page of spreadsheets appeared. Goddamn, it was all there. "Arnie," he breathed, "you genius. You did it." Just then, a trashcan crashed over nearby, the noise tearing through the night. Greg closed the program quickly and shut down the laptop. He listened intently, trying to discern what sort of animal might have made the noise. He waited, crouched on the floor until another sound reached his ears. No animal this time, he could clearly hear a shoe crunching on gravel.

There was a small shelf of cleaning supplies above his head. He moved silently, recapped the small jump drive and tucked it behind the bottle of bleach. Then he flipped off the inside light and paused, before slowly opening the door and stepping out. He shut it gently and jumped off the short deck into the reedy dunes, waiting.

Once the man had reached the bottom of the deck and was walking up to the bathhouse, Greg could see his silhouette in the light from the deck. It was the aging hippie he'd met that afternoon when he was out kayaking around the sound. A harmless fellow, he'd offered Greg part of his day's catch in exchange for a game of cribbage. Greg took a deep breath. Only four of the campsites were filled that night as the park was finishing up its regular season. He didn't know if they'd let him stay on at the camp once the concession stand had closed but he figured he had a few days to figure out his next step. It would have to be a big one.

Monday and Tuesday he spent his time cleaning the bathhouse, concession stand and boat launching area. He swept and scrubbed and saved what food he could. Most he packaged up to give to the local food bank while the rest he stored in a tiny corner of the large, commercial refrigerator. The ferryboat captain came on Wednesday and together they loaded all of the materials that were to be sent back to the mainland. The public buildings were all closed and locked and he let Greg know that the electricity would stay on and the volunteers' restroom would remain open until the threat of freezing came, then they'd be shut as well and everyone would be expected to vacate the island.

Greg waved good-bye to the captain and then set out to walk the island once more. He checked out the long run of campsites that paralleled the shore but it was clear that everyone else had left. There was an interesting sort of freedom to the place, an emptiness that he didn't think he'd ever experienced. In the city and at college he had never really been alone and he wasn't entirely sure what he thought of the situation. He wondered if he should take off his clothes and dance around naked or something just because he could. The whole thing was more than a little unnerving. The time had come to make a plan and follow it through.

On Thursday morning he retrieved the USB drive from where he'd stashed it and set about studying the information Arnie had collected. Knowing Arnie, he wasn't surprised by its thoroughness. The reach of the Warren crime family was deep. Walt and his brother James had been running the numbers game in the city as well as the surrounding counties in addition to what appeared to be the bulk of the loan sharking and drug sales. Jay Warren's part of the enterprise was considerably darker and included areas Greg had known nothing about. Enforcement seemed to be his first responsibility, breaking knees, legs, even families in an unending pressure to make people pay. In addition, Jay seemed to be in charge of a lot of heavy-duty weaponry that was traveling into the city and out to the surrounding towns in jaw-dropping numbers.

It was a wonder there hadn't been a militia style takeover in the area.

Greg found the lists of names that the report included to be even more interesting including city officials, a judge, an attorney from the DA's office as well as law clerks and even interns. The list of policemen involved was fairly short but it included one guy that he'd known, a brute named Gauthier who'd tossed out his share of gay slurs and roughed him up more than once. More dangerous though, was the fact that the list also included several people highly ranked in the force. He knew that there was no telling how and where their power would have reached.

Greg continued paging through the files, child pornography sales, the sale of migrant women, even what looked like a burgeoning business in importing slave labor. Jay Warren's dirty fingerprints were everywhere. After an hour and a half, he'd had enough. He tucked the drive back up with the cleaning supplies and set out on foot again. He considered getting into the ocean, hoping that the surf would wash away some of the filth he felt but the air and water were both too cool. When walking didn't prove to be enough, he got in the kayak and paddled around through the various channels until his arms were ready to fall off. As the sun was setting in a blaze of reds and pinks, he sat on one of the tallest dunes looking out over the sound. Finally his thoughts had quieted, except for one. He wished Arnie were sitting beside him, telling him what to do. But as he sat, the sun and the colors fading, there was no sense of a hand on his shoulder. He was as alone mentally as he was physically, and that was the most frightening thing he'd learned all day.

CHAPTER TWENTY-EIGHT

"*I* won't be long," Cindy called over her shoulder to Ray as they walked into her apartment.

"Take your time. We can let the rush hour traffic get out of town first." Ray went into the kitchen and filled a glass with water. The week had been less than productive. He and Cindy were both ready for a change of scenery. The local cops had followed through on Gray's ID but hadn't been able to locate Turner, even after three days. Defeat was in the air and it was suffocating. They had stopped by his place first where he'd grabbed his go-bag and stuffed it with a windbreaker and an extra sweater. They'd parked his car on the street outside Cindy's place and gone inside for her to gather up what she needed. He took a long drink as he walked into the living room. "Hey, there's a message on the machine. Want me to get it?"

"Sure," Cindy called from the bathroom.

"Hello," a rich southern accent filled the room. "This is Ada Loving and I'm calling from Hammock's Beach State Park. I'm sorry I missed your call earlier. We're working on shutting everything down so we don't keep someone in the office regularly. I can tell you that the ferry made its final runs last weekend since we're done for the season. There's just one outhouse style restroom that stays open through the winter, the rest is locked up, I'm afraid. You're welcome to come on down and see the place, but you'll have to find your own transportation out to the island. Call me back if there's anything I can do!"

Cindy emerged from the back room as she pulled the zipper shut on the small duffle bag. She grinned at Ray. "Our own transportation? What do you think that means? A boat?"

"Well, I guess. You know anything about boats?"

Cindy laughed and shook her head, "Sorry dude, city girl. What about you? Were you a boy scout or anything like that?"

Ray laughed and caught her up in a quick hug. "As a matter of fact I was, an Eagle Scout." He shrugged, "I spent one summer kayaking on a lake up north, but that's about it as far as boats go."

"Well, it's more than me. I've been camping before, once. "She paused. "When I was 10. Besides, we can probably just hire someone to take us out there, if he's still there, that is." Cindy looked pointedly at where the listening device was located and then shrugged without saying anymore.

Ray grabbed up her bag while she gathered the keys and went around turning off lights. "Let's hit it then." He grinned and pulled the door shut behind them. They had called ahead so Ray waited in the car outside while Cindy ran in to Lulu's to pick up their food. She was pleased to see CB behind the bar wrangling what looked like three or four takeout orders.

"One of those mine?" Cindy grinned and reached her hand out as he settled the bags on the counter.

"I thought I recognized that name on the order. How are you doing, Agent?"

"It's Cindy." She shook his hand, smiled, then leaned on the counter.

"How's the big case? The manhunt? I was so surprised when that other guy came in here asking about those two men. They're really going all out on it, huh?"

WHO WE MIGHT BE

"Someone else was in asking?"

He nodded, "Yeah, not but, like a day later I think. He told me he owed the guy some money, wasn't really looking too hard for him, you know?" CB laughed.

"Can you remember what he looked like?"

CB shook his head. "Sorry, no, I remember he was an older guy, ordered a tuna melt with fries but I don't remember the face, I'm afraid."

"A tuna melt guy, huh? What am I, CB?"

He laughed back. "You're the good looking mac and cheese, boss," he grinned as he handed over the bag. "Your face, I remember!"

Another customer had arrived to pick up their food so Cindy gave him a quick wave and headed back to the car.

She set the bag of food on the floor at her feet before fastening her seat belt. As Ray eased the car into the southbound traffic, she made a quick call to check on Gray, then pulled out napkins and plastic utensils. "I have no idea how you're going to eat this and drive." She laughed, looking over at Ray.

"I'm an old pro." He took one of the napkins and tucked it into the top of his shirt before flattening a second one out on his lap. "Ready."

Cindy opened the takeout container and settled it on his lap, the plastic spoon sticking out on the side. "It's pretty hot so give it a minute." She pulled the second container out and began opening its lid as well. "Guess who was in to see the bartender CB, asking about Hanes and Lowe?"

Ray whipped his head toward her. "Turner?"

She shrugged and blew gently on the first bite of food. "He said an older guy who got a tuna melt. My guess would be Turner, wouldn't yours?" She touched her lip to the first bite but it was still blazing hot. "Yikes!" She put her hand on his arm as he was lifting the first bite up. "Careful, it's still…"

She watched in horror as he put a heaping spoonful in his mouth. "Whu?" He looked at her questioningly but proceeded to chew the bite as though there was nothing to it. "You okay?"

Cindy shook her head and continued to blow on each bite of the food. "Feel like some music?" Cindy asked as she checked the battery level on her phone.

Ray stretched out his arms and then relaxed back into his seat. "That'd be great. How far do you think we should try to get tonight?"

Cindy stowed the empty containers, then hooked the phone into the car's stereo system and turned it to a manageable volume level. "I checked over the map before we left and there are a couple of different routes but the most direct one goes past DC. Do you think we could get that far tonight, maybe a little past it?"

Ray reached over to the radio dial and turned the volume up a hair. "Sounds good to me, DC it is. Why don't you see if you can get us a hotel reservation somewhere and that will give us a target to head for." He began humming along with the tune as she pulled her tablet out of her bag and began searching for a reservation.

CHAPTER TWENTY-NINE

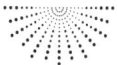

*W*hen Pete arrived back at his apartment he laid his bag down and threw himself onto the old sofa. The springs groaned but he sunk his head in his hands and ignored it. Fuck, what the fuck had he been thinking? Now he'd be stuck dodging the cops all week. But really, what were the odds that some old pawnshop guy would know the agent? People were always saying that Pittsburgh was more small-town than city but he'd never believed it, until today that is. Shit.

The next few days Pete worked close to home, slipping out only for food. He checked in on the agent's apartment bugs and tracker but there didn't seem to be much happening there. If what his source in the DA's office said was true, the FBI was going flat out trying to find something more on Jay Warren before the case went forward. The agent seemed to be getting up early, coming home late and falling into bed each night. In the meantime he'd been solidifying plans with some of their old distributors. There'd been no more demands from James Warren and for that he was grateful. He'd gone over the pick-up plans with the Morelli brothers until he was convinced they could handle it.

Late Thursday afternoon he was staring at the mediocre

contents of his refrigerator when he heard movement in the agent's apartment. He grabbed his last beer and moved closer to his computer. He could hear the bitch and her agent boyfriend walking into the living room. Then a thick southern accent came from what sounded like an old fashioned answering machine. What kind of idiot still had a landline? He listened carefully but had no idea why they'd be listening to someone talk about some state park. Were they planning a trip? Now? Then the two of them left.

He sank down onto the couch as he took a long draw on his beer. Was the FBI giving up on the Warren case, letting their agents take vacation time? It just didn't jibe with what he'd been hearing. He went downstairs to pick up some dinner, then came back up and settled in front of his computer. The tracker on the agent's car showed them leaving the city and getting onto the highway going east. He checked on their progress throughout the evening until they seemed to stop just south of the DC beltway. It had taken him a while to find the park that he'd heard mentioned on the answering machine but he still had no idea why they'd be heading there. He rewound his recording of their conversation and listened to it twice more before focusing on one line. "If he's still there." Who were they looking for, he wondered? It was late but he risked making a call to his source in the DA's office. It was a long shot, but maybe he'd know what they were working on.

"Do you know what time it is?"

"Sorry, I'll make it quick. Listen, you know that agent I was talking to you about? Do you know what she and her boyfriend have been working on, what part of the Warren case?"

"Not really, they were kind of peripheral as far as I could tell. Last I heard I think they were focusing in on Jay's accountant's death. Now hang up and don't call me again, ever. Are we clear?"

The phone clicked off before he could answer but he'd gotten the message all right. If they were focused on the accountant was it Hanes they were looking for? Shit, if Hanes was there, he had to get to him first. He tossed the food scraps and the rest of his beer in the trash and hurried around picking up the few clothes that were clean and stuffing them into a worn roller bag. He plugged the location of the park into his GPS system and set off, dialing Tony as he maneuvered his way through the city.

"Yup, what's up? Kinda late don't you think?"

"Shut up you, moron. Listen, I have to go out of town tonight so I'm counting on you to handle the pick up tomorrow. Are you sure you're set?"

"Of course, you've gone over it with us a dozen times. We're good."

"When you get back, go to the safe house and park the car in the garage. You can slip the key under my door and I'll take care of everything when I get back."

"All right, you got it. I'll text you once we're back."

Pete clicked off and tossed the phone on the seat beside him. He had the road to himself and he made good time. When he thought he couldn't go any further, he pulled into a rest area off the highway outside of Richmond, Virginia and fell asleep in his back seat. Once the morning light filled the car, he woke up and scrubbed his hand down his face. He stepped out of the car and made his way into the rest area to piss and splash cold water on his face. One of the booths in the food court was cooking bacon so he wandered over and ordered some breakfast. He pulled out his computer and checked on the agent's tracker. It was 6:30 A.M. and they were still in the same spot. Good, he thought. He had about four hours to go and at least a two-hour head start.

CHAPTER THIRTY

When they'd fallen into bed the night before, Ray and Cindy had left the heavy, outer drape slightly open. Now the morning light was knifing into her eyes with the reminder that they were indeed working. At least they weren't on anyone's clock but their own. She could feel Ray stirring as well so she leaned over and spooned around his back. It was so warm and perfect, why did they have to move? But after only a few minutes, it was clear that they were awake for the day. Cindy slipped into the bathroom first, not wanting to ruin the morning with her ridiculous bed hair and bad breath. She heard Ray calling from the door.

"Hey, they've got breakfast in the restaurant downstairs, want to take a few minutes more to eat?"

"Sure," she called back, "I need coffee immediately."

It was a limited menu but the coffee was passable and they were in the car before eight. Cindy drove while Ray called the office. She could hear his half of the conversation but it wasn't enough to understand fully so she waited for him to explain. Ray shut off the phone and set it on the center console.

"So what's happening? Any word on Turner?"

"No, and it's ridiculous it's taking this long. But get this, the agents watching Jay Warren's condo went through their check of the place and someone had broken into his storage area."

"They didn't see anyone?"

"No, unfortunately." He shrugged. "You know how it gets when a detail goes on too long. Anyway, the money that was there is now missing and guess who's on the road?"

Cindy looked over at Ray, "how much? You mean the agency knew there was money there? Did you know that?"

Ray shook his head. "Me, no, I had no idea. But I guess there was about a $100,000 there when he was arrested so they decided to leave it in place and see if anyone came for it."

"So who's on the road?"

"It seems the Morelli brothers left the city about an hour ago heading east on the turnpike."

"Where do you think they're going? Is someone tailing them at least?"

"Yep, two guys from down my hall are on it. They're planning on sticking with them."

"I really wish I knew where Turner is." Cindy twisted her hand around the steering wheel in frustration. "I hate the idea of Gray leaving the hospital with him unaccounted for."

Ray nodded, "Well, when I talked to the detective, he told me he was going to request a detail to keep an eye on him for a little bit." He shrugged apologetically, "they've only got funds to run it through the weekend but we should be back by then and hopefully they'll have Turner in the bag by then too."

It took another five hours to get to Jacksonville, the town they'd seen noted in both men's financial records. They took the time to drive around to the branch bank where Hanes had withdrawn his money, but no one remembered anything about the transaction and the video tapes had long since been recorded over.

Ray took over the wheel as they got back into the car, scorching now even in the late afternoon. Cindy threw her purse in on the floor and settled into her seat.

The GPS system faltered at first but finally got them heading southeast toward the park. The afternoon was wearing on and they were relieved to arrive at the park finally. It was situated just outside a small town called Swansboro but when they found the visitor center closed and locked, they returned to town. An outfitters' shop was located along the waterfront there and although business seemed to be pretty dead, the small shop was open.

A young woman with short blonde hair tied up in a bandanna, was seated behind the glass counter. One wall was filled with fishing equipment and photos of prize catches while another wall was lined with tall kayaks and boasted its own set of beautiful photographs. "Hi there, can I help y'all?" The young woman beamed at them.

Both Cindy and Ray pulled out their folded badges and laid them on the counter in front of her. Ray spoke first. "Good afternoon, we're from the FBI and we're trying to get some information about Hammock's Beach State Park. We drove over to the visitors' center but it looked as though it's all locked up."

"Yeah," she nodded, "they closed everything up there earlier this week. I think the ferry made a run over on Wednesday to bring back supplies and stuff but they're all done for now."

Cindy spoke up next as they pocketed their ID's. "Is anyone else out there?"

The woman shrugged, "Gee, I don't think so." She hopped off her seat and headed toward the back of the shop. "Let me ask Jason, I think he took the ferry over on the last run. Give me a sec."

"God I hope we didn't drive all the way down here for nothing," Cindy moaned as she bent at the waist to try and ease out some of the kinks. She straightened then as an older man in cut-off shorts and a faded baseball cap followed the young woman out. Cindy and

Ray reached for their badges again but the man waved them off. "Hi folks, I'm Jason Stamps. What can I do for you?"

Cindy and Ray both shook hands with him, then Cindy continued. "Mr. Stamps, we understand that you drove the ferry out to the island on Wednesday this week, is that right?"

"Yep, at the end of the season we haul out the perishables that are left, turn them over to the food bank here in town and then we store a lot of the summer gear at a warehouse on the other side of town." He gestured over his shoulder. "Did you need something from there?"

"No," Cindy shook her head, "we're looking for someone. We thought they might still be out on the island. We were hoping to talk with them."

The man took off his cap and ran his fingers through his thinning hair. "Wow, that is some coincidence. The tourists are all gone of course, but there is a guy out there who was running the concession stand for them during this last month. In fact, I just got back from running some city guy out there, said he needed to talk to him. Did he do something wrong?"

Cindy and Ray looked at each other in alarm. "Can you describe the 'city guy' to us? Did he give you a name?"

The man scratched his forehead before resettling the cap on his head. "No, I don't think I got a name, seemed friendly enough, you know, paid me in cash in fact. It's just a quick run out there in a skiff." He raised his hand to about five-eight and continued. "I'd say he was about this tall, grayish hair, kind of wiry you know, not athletic but not fat either."

Ray pulled out his phone and paged through the photos until he found the array that the detective had sent to Gray in the hospital. He turned it toward the boatman and began paging through them again, just as he had earlier. The reaction was the same. On the fifth photo the man's hand pointed. "Yep, that's him." He looked at the young woman and back to the agents. "Can you tell me what's going on? Who's the bad guy here?"

Cindy turned to Ray and then asked the man, "We've got to get out there, now. Can you take us out?"

"Sure. I told that guy I'd be back to pick him up just before sunset." He looked at his watch. "I told him around 6:30."

Ray and Cindy looked at their watches. It was 5:15. "How long does it take?"

"Well, you're in a hurry, I can make it in about 20 minutes, provided you don't mind a rough ride."

Cindy and Ray exchanged a look but there really wasn't any alternative. Ray pulled a fifty out of his wallet, "will this be enough? I don't really know what boats cost."

The man shook his head and declined the money. "Nah, nah, if there's something going on, I'd rather help than wait to hear about it. I'll meet you down at the end of the dock in about five minutes."

Ray and Cindy thanked the young woman and headed toward the car. "How the hell did Pete Turner get here?"

"Did we lead him here?" Ray asked.

"How? He seems to have beaten us here. What the hell's going on, Ray?"

He opened the trunk and began assembling the small rifle he'd thrown in the car at the last minute. He looked over at Cindy. "What do you think, vests?"

She nodded, and they both donned the close fitting vests. Cindy fastened on her shoulder harness, checked her gun and placed it in the holster as Ray followed with the same motions. "How rough do you think is rough?" Ray slammed the trunk shut and walked with her down toward the dock.

"I guess we'll find out soon enough."

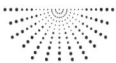

CHAPTER THIRTY-ONE

*P*ete arrived in Swansboro got a bite to eat at a fast food joint and then walked the little stretch of street that led to the water and held a few shops. A large outfitters' shop was an easy first stop, the proprietor a fount of information. Sure enough, it appeared Hanes was on the island and had been there for more than a month. He was going by a different name but the description was spot on. Pete was even more pleased when he offered the man $200 bucks, and he agreed to take him out to the island on his boat. In hindsight, he figured that fee must have been too high because the man's face lit up quickly at the prospect. But what the hell, it wasn't like it was his money since he'd borrowed some off the stack before he'd given it to Tony. The Outfitter guy made quick work of getting the boat ready. Pete left his car where it was and tossed his jacket on over his gun, zipping the bottom of it before making his way down to the end of the dock.

The man nodded approvingly. "Good thing you've got that windbreaker. It's gonna get pretty windy on our way out there."

Pete said nothing, just stepped into the boat and took a seat in the front. Within a few minutes they'd gotten beyond the no-wake zone of the little harbor and out into more open water. The man cranked up the motor and the boat began skidding across the top of the small waves, its front end slamming down over and over again until Pete felt like he was either going to die or kill someone else. He looked sharply at the man driving the boat.

The man looked surprised. "What, too fast? You said you were in a hurry, didn't you?"

Pete gritted his teeth together before he croaked out, "not that much of one!" The driver could see his white knuckled grip on the sides of the seat so he eased back on the throttle and cut out some of the jarring until they arrived at the small dock.

Pete stepped out onto the dock and was reaching for the rope that dangled off the front of the small boat.

"I'll be back for you around sunset, say like 6:30 or so?" It was a question but he was already backing the boat out and away before Pete had a chance to answer. He thought about pulling out his gun but the boat was moving away quickly and there was no way to watch the man anyway. He looked around suddenly more aware of the odd situation he'd put himself in. A kayak lay upside down near the end of the dock but he paid it little attention. Ahead, there were signs that pointed to a bathhouse and observation area as well as picnic shelters and campsites. He spotted a small bathroom off to the side and noticed that it was open but once inside he realized it was really just an outhouse and he stormed out in disgust. Most everything else seemed to be either straight ahead or off to his left somewhere but there was no indication of how far. Shit, he didn't even have on decent shoes. Goddamn Greg Hanes.

Pete took off walking, swatting at the occasional mosquito, his neckline growing damp in the late afternoon heat. Within minutes he'd had to ditch the windbreaker, leaving it hanging on the branch of a nearby tree. How in the hell was he going to find this guy before sundown, he wondered? The path carried him finally to the long, low bathhouse which lay between him and the oceanfront. It had a wide, wooden walkway leading up to it but was nestled into the dunes on either side. He tried the front doors and then walked around on the surrounding deck, not finding a way in. He stopped and listened but could hear nothing other than the roar of the surf and the wind in the dune grasses. Across the wide path was the walkway up to the observation area so he tried that next, but it too was locked. Shit, what now?

Pete turned and walked down toward the long row of campsites, looking for one that appeared to be occupied. What did they call this anyway, primitive camping, was that what the sign had said? How in the hell had Hanes managed to live here for more than a month? He kept scanning the area until he spotted what appeared to be the end spot. Shit, they were all empty. Where the fuck was Hanes?

There was no way he'd find the asshole this way. Sooner or later, he'd have to use the bathroom, right? He turned and retraced his steps, determined to wait by the outhouse until the man returned. The smell made him want to kill the motherfucker even more.

CHAPTER THIRTY-TWO

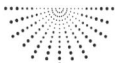

riday morning arrived clear and sunny with a hint of
the summer's heat in the air rather than the fall chill
that Greg had been getting used to. It felt like an omen in a way, a
day to make a decision, to start fresh. He decided he would take the
morning to enjoy the island, a meandering walk gathering a few
seashells and trying to imprint the look of the place on his memory
before rowing over to the mainland after lunch. In hindsight it had
proven to be a good hiding place, and for a city kid he felt like he'd
managed pretty well. He was strong, completely healed from the
beating and feeling better physically than he had in years.

After returning to his campsite, Greg put together a lunch from
what was left and tucked it into the small string bag. The rest of his
things he carried back across the island and packed into the kayak,
which was lying upside down along the ferry dock. With a mix of
relief and resignation he headed up to the tallest of the three dunes.
Once settled into his favorite spot, a flattened area where he had
nearly a 360-degree view of the island, he took out his lunch and
ate slowly. It was too far to see the mainland of course, but he could
see the various islands that filled the channel as well as the broad,
blue emptiness of the Atlantic. The air still held a bit of summer's

warmth. He grew drowsy as he lay looking up into the cloud dotted sky.

Greg heard the motorboat before he saw it, inching its way out through the narrow channel. He picked up the cheap binoculars that he'd found and recognized Jason, the ferryboat captain, at the helm. He was ready to stand up and wave when he caught sight of the passenger huddled miserably in the front of the boat. He dropped to the sand and began scrambling to put everything back into the string bag before shimmying back to the edge of the dune where he had a clear view but couldn't be seen from below. How in God's name had Pete Turner found him?

Greg lay on his stomach watching as the small skiff pulled up to the dock and Turner stepped out. It looked as if maybe a quick argument was going on as Jason quickly backed away from the dock. Greg felt a small satisfaction in seeing the bewildered look on Turner's face as he took off walking in the direction of the island's main buildings.

Greg saw Turner look briefly at the kayak but thankfully he didn't turn it over. Greg scrambled down from the dune and took the quickest route to his former campsite, the last one in the main set. He took a few minutes to kick sand around and do his best to disguise his recent use of the site. With his gear out of site and the USB drive safe in the locked concession, he made his way back to higher ground and continued watching as Turner moved between the buildings and then headed toward him. If he could just get to the kayak before Turner spotted him, he could slip out quietly and row back in among the smaller barrier islands. Once it was dark, he'd head to shore and try to get to his car.

Suddenly, it felt as though there were a lot of 'ifs' in play. Because of the long inlet, he was forced to move toward Turner before he could cut back away from him across the island to the dock. The dunes were lower here and more irregular so he had to move in fits and starts, darting from one grass covered hill to another until he'd made it around the inlet. Then it was a matter of moving across the width of the island toward the flat area that overlooked the sound. With slightly better cover for most of the way, he was able to stand up straight and run through the tufted hills. He paused in the last cover that the dunes offered, lay flat and pulled out his binoculars again. It worried him that he couldn't see Turner and he hoped that the man was still walking down the long line of campsites looking for him. He stowed the binoculars back in the string bag and crouched, ready to move. Part of him thought he was hearing another motorboat but he was so intent on his goal that he ignored the sound. The roar grew louder then and he wondered, who else would be coming out there? He got to the kayak and flipped it over easily, tossed the string bag in ahead of him and lowered the front end off the dock. As he set the other end down and climbed in, he suddenly heard Turner running toward him, his feet pounding on the wooden boards, yelling at him to stop.

.

CHAPTER THIRTY-THREE

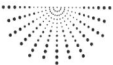

*A*s the two agents approached the end of the dock, clad in full gear with guns, bulletproof vests and FBI emblazoned across their chests, Jason thought twice about his offer to take them out. "Wow, you're not messing around."

Ray tried to be reassuring. "It's just precautionary." He stepped down into the skiff and then reached a hand up for Cindy. The two of them barely fit on the metal bench and the boat dipped back and forth as they tried to settle in. As soon as they were ready he called back over his shoulder, "We're good," and the boat pulled out slowly.

Jason worked the throttle and steered easily as they moved out of the no-wake zone. He didn't know if they'd have any more of a stomach for the ride than the other guy had but he figured he'd soon find out.

The boat was really moving, bouncing against each small wave as they moved forward into the channel. Ray and Cindy clung tightly to the sides and each other, but they didn't ask him to slow down. Knowing that Turner was out there ahead of them made speed essential. The sun was still high enough for them to see the outlines of the various islands but there were clouds building in the west and they would hasten the growing darkness.

The captain was as good as his word. Before long the island was coming in to view. Jason pointed out the ferry dock with its high, easy steps that tourists piled onto each day in the summer. But they were coming around to the lower side, where access was provided for smaller motorboats as well as kayaks and canoes. As they grew closer, it looked as though there was a boat in the water already and Turner seemed to be running toward it. It wasn't clear whether either man had spotted them yet, but they could hear Turner yelling.

"Get back here, Hanes, you asshole! I just want to talk to you."

But Greg's head was down and he was working as quickly as he could to turn the craft around so that he could head out into the channel. Suddenly a quick explosion sounded and his left arm was slammed back taking his body with it, the paddle dropping into the boat in front of him. They could see Turner getting closer, nearly upon him as he tried frantically to get the paddle into the water one handed.

"Hanes, you bastard, I said stop," the man yelled as he raised his gun again, this time at nearly point blank range. Turner aimed it at Greg and fired just as he managed to wield the paddle up in the air and bat at the gun in his hand. There was a flash of light and he fell backward into the bottom of the small craft.

Once they heard the first gunshot, Cindy climbed backward toward Jason and pulled him down as far as he could go. She had her weapon drawn. "Get us as close as you can, but stay down."

"Stop, FBI!" Cindy yelled.

Ray pulled the rifle up and was trying to site along the barrel, even as the water near the dock caused the boat to lurch. Another shot rang out and he rose up to take aim. He saw Turner pivot their way and the next bullet hit Ray in the shoulder, knocking him back into the water. Turner aimed again at the incoming skiff but before he could shoot, Cindy fired quickly and Turner went down just as Jason threw a loop of rope around the post and reached to pull Ray back into the boat. The bullet hit Turner in the center of his chest and knocked him down on the deck. On the skiff, Ray was moving slowly and spitting out water but the vest had done its job. Cindy leapt up onto the deck and moved forward, her gun still aimed at Pete Turner's prone form. But there was no movement at all. The man was dead. She holstered her gun and called out to the boat.

Jason raced forward and reached down to grab the rope that lay in the water. He pulled the kayak close and with Cindy's help, they were able to pick up Greg and lay him on the wooden dock. Jason ran to his boat and came back with a first aid kit. Ray had followed behind as quickly as he could and he whipped off his belt and began fastening it around Greg's leg. It was bleeding as though one of the shots had hit an artery. As the two men worked on him, Cindy pulled out her phone and dialed 911.

"Hello, this is Agent Cindy O'Brien with the FBI. We've got multiple gunshot wounds on a victim out on Bear Island. We need a medevac chopper immediately, I repeat, immediately." She paused to listen, agreed and then returned just as Jason was pulling out a shiny foil square and unfolding the thermal blanket around him. "How is he?"

Ray stood, peeling off his vest and rubbing at the spot on his shoulder. "I'm not sure. We've got the bleeding stopped in his leg for now and Jason's keeping pressure on the shoulder, but I don't know. It'll depend on how long the chopper takes."

Just then Cindy noticed that Greg seemed to be coming around. He tried to sit up but the pain shot through him again and he fell back.

"Lie still, help's on the way." Cindy leaned over and rested her hand on his shoulder. "Are you Gregory Hanes?" she asked.

Greg nodded feebly and tried to reach for the chain around his neck. She helped him ease it off and noticed that it held a single key. His voice was growing faint. "cleaning... drive." She looked up at Ray, uncertain what any of it meant. He shrugged and took over for Jason, keeping pressure on the shoulder wound as the older man rested. It felt like years before the faint sound of a helicopter grew loud enough to be heard above the surf.

Once the chopper team had stabilized Greg they prepared to lift off. "You go with him," Cindy called to Ray over the sound of the blades. "Get yourself checked out too. I'll come find you both once I'm finished here." Ray nodded reluctantly, and climbed in beside the stretcher that held Greg Hanes.

After they lifted off, Cindy was on the phone again, this time calling in a forensic team from the nearest FBI office. She waited by Turner's body as Jason left in the skiff and retuned forty-five minutes later with the ferry and the needed agents on board. Night was falling quickly so lights were set up and small teams set out across the island in different directions. With Hanes's key in hand, Cindy headed to the out buildings, checking out the bathhouse first. The electricity was still working so she flipped on lights as she went in. She searched the women's side first but found nothing, then moved into the men's section. She walked past the benches for changing and along the row of shower stalls but nothing appeared out of place.

Cleaning, Cindy thought, what did that mean? Was he cleaning in here when Turner showed up? She continued looking but didn't see anything. Finally, she approached the concessions building and tried the key again. It was a small area, just a counter and low refrigerator. She noticed above that was a high shelf that appeared to hold cleaning supplies. She moved toward it and reached up with a gloved hand, pushing aside a gallon bottle of bleach. Then she spotted it, a small figurine that looked like a space man. She opened an evidence bag and dropped it in. Once it was protected inside, Cindy pulled on it gently and the head came off to reveal a USB drive.

"Well, I'll be damned."

CHAPTER THIRTY-FOUR

*I*t was after midnight before the team finished and Cindy was able to ride back over to the mainland. The ferry proved to be a lot more comfortable than the skiff had been, but fatigue was setting in and she gave it little thought. All of the energy she had left was focused on her left pocket where a tiny spaceman held a universe of possibility. Once the agents were all off she stepped up to Jason and held out her hand.

"I can't thank you enough, captain." She gestured at the crew around her that was departing.

The man smiled and shook her hand warmly, a small laugh escaping. "I said I'd rather watch than wait and hear about it, didn't I? Guess I might think twice about that next time!" he laughed. "You take care now, agent, and come back sometime when you're free to relax."

Cindy nodded and moved off. Her phone had rung just as they were docking, but she'd let it go, taking a moment to gather Hanes's personal items before moving toward her car. She nodded goodbye to the other agents, stowed the gear and slipped into the driver's seat before hitting the call back function. It was picked up immediately.

"Ray, how are you?"

"Good, I'm good, just a bad bruise. It looks like Hanes is going to make it too. They patched his shoulder up before taking him into surgery for his leg. He's still there now, but one of the nurses just came out to tell me they're optimistic."

"That's a relief," she paused. "Ray, he may turn out to be incredibly important. Where are you now?"

"What do you mean? I'm in a town called Kinston, nurse said it's about an hour from Swansboro."

"I'll be there as soon as I can. I can tell you more once I arrive."

"Okay, drive safe."

He clicked off and she tossed the phone on the passenger seat. The roads out of the area were small and empty this time of night, but finally she spotted a rest area ahead. From her bag in the back she dug out fresh clothes and went into the women's room to clean up and change. A quick stop for coffee and a power bar and she was back on the road. The emergency sign lit up the entrance to the hospital and made it easy for her to find her way. She took a minute to grab Ray's bag as well as the one that held Greg Hanes's few things. A tired looking nurse was sitting at the duty desk when she walked in.

The woman managed a weak smile in spite of the fatigue. "Can I help you find someone?"

Cindy set the bags on the floor beside her and pulled out her badge. "I'm agent Cindy O'Brien and I'm looking for..."

Just then Ray appeared from around the corner, blood stained clothes beneath a bright smile.

Cindy picked up the bags, following Ray around to a small waiting room. "I'd hug you but I'm still pretty filthy." He clung to her hand.

Cindy smiled and held up the duffle. She leaned in to kiss him, resting her hand on his shoulder. "I'm glad to see you. How about some clean clothes?" She gestured behind her.

While he was getting cleaned up, Cindy went back to talk with the nurse. "Can you tell me how Greg Hanes is doing? I understand he's in surgery?"

The woman nodded. "They just finished up. He's being moved to recovery now."

"And the leg?" Cindy held her breath.

"A lot of rehab is what he's looking at, but they saved the leg. Good thing the chopper made such good time."

Cindy nodded and returned to the waiting room. She reached her hand into her pocket and fingered the edge of the plastic evidence bag as she waited.

Finally Ray emerged looking tired but clean. He sat on the bench beside her and leaned in for a minute. "Did anyone ever tell you agent, you're a hell of a shot?"

Cindy laughed, "only all of my instructors. They cried when I went into computers."

"I can see why." He smiled and sat up straighter. "So, what did you find?"

Cindy reached into her pocket and pulled out the small figurine. Ray looked at her quizzically. "Legos?"

She held it up and popped off the small head, revealing the USB drive. "I can't wait to talk to Hanes and find out what's on this puppy." She returned it to her pocket and turned to face him again. "What's the word on the Morelli brothers, heard anything?"

He nodded. "Yep, they just caught them coming out of Philly in an old station wagon loaded with drugs. The locals picked up the supplier too, some old crook named Smokey. And guess what? They discovered about the money he was holding."

"Yes," she barked out, her hand in a tight fist pump. "I love it."

Just then the night duty nurse came around the corner. "He's coming around if you'd like to see him." They followed her down the hallway and past the emergency area to where the post-op patients were supervised. He was in the last bed with bandages peeking out from both the top and the bottom of the thin, white blanket. He looked so peaceful that they hated to disturb him.

Finally, Greg's eyes opened and seemed to come into focus. He looked toward the water glass and Ray reached it to him, touching the straw to his lips. He sipped slowly and then leaned his head back against the pillow before taking a deep breath. "So, am I under arrest?"

Ray and Cindy laughed, both of them shaking their heads. Ray carefully rested a hip on the side of the bed. "No, we're not arresting you. We're just glad to see you in one piece," Ray waggled his head, "uh, more or less."

Cindy pulled out the evidence bag holding the drive. "What can you tell us about this?"

The look of relief that washed over Greg's face was startling. "Oh, thank God. I was so afraid it would be lost in all of this." He gestured at the medical setting around them.

"So what's on it?" Cindy asked, tucking it back into her pocket.

"Everything," he breathed out, "every Goddamned thing. Arnie," he paused and the pain on his face was clear. "He told me he was looking for a way out. I had no idea what he'd done or where it was but somehow," he shrugged his shoulders and winced in pain. "It was like he led me to it."

"What do you mean by everything?" asked Ray.

Greg smiled. "All of it, the deals, the cons, names, places, amounts, every Goddamn thing you'd need to know." His eyes were drifting closed.

Cindy took Greg's free hand and squeezed it tight. "Is there anyone we can call?" But it was clear that he'd gone under again. The agents left his bag with the duty nurse and made plans to return the next day. She waved them off with directions to a nearby hotel. They pulled into the lot, registered and picked up keys without saying much, carried in the bags and dropped as one onto the wide bed.

"Helluva day, wouldn't you say, Agent O'Brien?"

Cindy grinned, "Yup, helluva day, Agent Sanchez." They took off their shoes and climbed under the covers, the evidence bag still tucked in Cindy's pocket.

CHAPTER THIRTY-FIVE

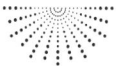

*R*ay and Cindy awoke to a gray, rainy Saturday morning but they didn't mind. They splurged on room service and took turns in the shower. While Ray finished, Cindy opened up her laptop and plugged in the small drive. She watched as page after page appeared. She was studying it, marveling, when Ray stepped out of the bathroom. "You look like the cat that swallowed the canary. Is it really all that?"

"It's unbelievable is what it is. Arnie Lowe was a genius. I don't know how he got away with it, but the man kept a record of any transaction that he was aware of. Plus, look at this." Cindy opened up a new page and Ray watched as a detailed list of names appeared. "He listed every name he learned as well as the role they played in the organization. Look, here are names from the DA's office."

"Christ, no wonder they were able to get the charges reduced."

"Yep, and here's a judge as well. They might have had the whole Jay Warren trial sealed up in a week."

Ray picked up a cinnamon roll, took a bite. "Do we need to be careful bringing this into our office? Have you found any FBI agents on the list?"

"No," Cindy sipped at her coffee and shook her head. "I've read all the way through and I think our office is clean. Still, I'd rather deliver it in person than trust any electronic transmission."

"I agree," Ray nodded. "Let's finish up and go visit Hanes, see how he's feeling this morning."

Together Ray and Cindy walked up the long flights of stairs and made their way down the hallway to Greg Hanes's room. He was sitting up in bed and looking considerably better than he had the night before. "How's it going, Agents?" he called out as they approached.

Cindy smiled, "We're good. It's great to see you looking better, too."

Greg shifted his position in the bed slightly and winced, but his face held a rueful smile. He used his good shoulder to offer a small shrug. "I've been better, but, all in all, not dead is good. "

Ray pulled up the visitor's chair and motioned Cindy into it while he perched again on the side of the bed. "Are you up to answering a few questions?"

"I can try."

Ray started. "Before you left the restaurant where Jay Warren was shot, you'd been beaten pretty badly. Who did it and why, do you know?"

"Tony Morelli, the bastard, with some help from Jay. They wanted me to tell them where Marybeth was but I didn't know."

Cindy spoke up, "Why did you take off from the restaurant?"

Greg raked his hand through his shaggy hair, leaving bits of it standing on end. "I didn't know what to do to tell you the truth. I'd been doing surveillance for Jay Warren for years. I figured you'd arrest me right along with him." His shoulders sagged and his head dropped. "It was more than that though, I was embarrassed and sick that Marybeth would find out that I'd been working for him all that time."

"Were you given a choice?" Ray asked.

"Hah, a choice with Jay Warren? I was in debt and he made sure I stayed that way. Once they had me at that warehouse beating me up, I figured I was dead. I never expected to get away from him, so when the confusion happened at the restaurant, I just bolted. It seemed like my only choice at the time."

"Can you tell us about Arnie Lowe," Cindy asked, watching his face carefully. The melancholy was clear. He took his time in answering.

"I loved Arnie, so much. I knew he had another life but whatever time he could give me, I took. It about broke me when they killed him."

"Do you know who did it?"

Greg shook his head. "I don't know for sure but I suspect it was Pete Turner. It was his style. When I saw Arnie's wife and kids at the funeral it was sort of a double whammy, a reminder that he was gone but also that he'd never really been mine." He looked up at the agents, clear eyed. "Arnie Lowe was forced to work for the Warrens the same as me. He didn't deserve what he got. He was a good man, agents, a really good man."

Ray and Cindy could tell that he was tiring. "We've made plans for the hospital to fly you to Pittsburgh's Mercy hospital as soon as you're able to be moved. In the meantime, is there someone you'd like for us to call?"

Greg hadn't dared to use his cell phone in so long he almost didn't know what to say. They waited while he considered. Finally, he seemed to come to a decision. "Once I'm back in the city, I'll give Marybeth a call. For now could you just let her know I'm okay? I appreciate all you've done for me. I wouldn't be here if it wasn't for you two." They stood to go and Cindy squeezed his good shoulder one more time. "We'll see you back in the city."

Greg nodded and then dropped his head back against the

pillow. They pulled the door shut and headed back out to the car. Cindy got into the driver's side as Ray slid in beside her.

They drove the entire day, pausing only to eat and trade off drivers. Once they were just outside the city, Ray called his captain and arranged for him to meet them at the office. A skeleton crew was working the weekend, struggling to find what they could before the DA's abrupt deadline. They walked into the captain's office and shut the door.

"What's up here and why do you two look so ridiculous?"

Ray laughed, "You mean why do we look like we just woke up on Christmas morning? It's because we have." Cindy pulled the drive out of her pocket and handed the evidence bag over to the captain. "See that little spaceman there? He's going to win it all for us."

Ray grinned and Cindy took up the story. "Arnie Lowe had been looking for a way out of the Warren family business for a long time. He figured the best bet he had was information," she paused, "a lot of information. That drive contains the details on every operation as well as the names and dates of everyone involved. The DA's office wasn't scared to prosecute, they were bought."

"Son of a bitch," the captain yelled. "I knew there had to be something else going on." He grinned. "So who else knows?"

Ray answered, "just the two of us and Greg Hanes. He's lying in the hospital in Kinston, North Carolina. Pete Turner found him at a little park down there and took a couple of shots at him." He hooked his thumb toward Cindy. "Luckily, Agent O'Brien here is a much better shot than Turner. He's on a slab in Swansboro waiting for transport here, that is if anyone cares to haul his worthless body back." Ray shrugged.

"Captain," Cindy spoke up then, "We're going to need everyone. It's a long list and we're going to have to coordinate the arrests before word gets out about Turner. I can print you the list of names."

The captain stood and beamed at the two agents. "Christmas fucking morning it is, good work you two." Cindy clasped Ray's hand one more time before racing up the stairs to her desk.

CHAPTER THIRTY-SIX

On Monday morning, Janine was ushering the children out to play when Carolyn's phone rang. Once the children were outside and greeting Rusty, she picked up the phone to answer. "Good morning, Edward Clark Children's Center, how may I help you?"

"Dear, you won't believe it."

"Hi, Charlie? What's going on?"

"He's been arrested, the lawyers just called me."

"Who, Charlie, who's been arrested?"

"James Warren, that's who. He was picked up this morning along with a whole host of others, some police, a judge, even a few from the DA's office."

"Wow! So what does this mean for us? What did the lawyers say?" Carolyn held her breath, a desperate hope starting to form inside of her.

"It's over!" he chortled. "The whole blooming business is over. The estate is yours, all of the challenges have been tossed out."

"Oh, my God," she yelled, "This is amazing!"

By now Janine had heard the uproar and ducked her head back inside the classroom. "We'll talk soon, Charlie, a lot!" Carolyn clicked off the phone and began jumping up and down. She grabbed Janine, "It's over! The court challenge is done! That monster James Warren's been arrested along with his cronies!"

Carolyn grabbed the house phone and dialed Helen in the kitchen. "Helen, grab Rupert and come back here, quick!" She dropped the phone back onto the cradle and fell into the nearest chair.

Within moments, Rupert and Helen were rushing into the room, Angela trailing in their wake. "What's going on, Miss?" Rupert asked.

Carolyn moved quickly to hug Rupert, then Helen and Angela. "It's over! The court challenge has been dropped! The lawyers told Charlie we're free and clear!"

Suddenly they were all talking at once until Carolyn caught sight of the children on their way back in.

Helen began herding the adults back out, but she took a second to announce, "We're having champagne with lunch today!" Carolyn and Janine laughed before turning to greet the children and guiding them into the next activity. Once the children had gone, they stood in front of the big TV set in Janine's room and watched the news unfold.

A reporter was standing before a large, brick home on the city's east side. "*... of the home of James Warren, once the home of his brother, Walt Warren, who was killed in a plane crash early this year. We're being told that newly discovered records of the Warren family enterprises have led to a series of arrests that have rocked the city. Those taken into custody today include members of the Warren family as well as several police officers, a high ranking judge and several members of the District Attorney's office. In further developments, Jay Warren, once thought to have been killed in the same crash that took the life of his father, is now being charged with multiple counts of murder, including that of his father. More on this from...*" They clicked off the set and dropped down onto the sofa.

"Unbelievable," Janine shook her head. "You are now, unequivocally a bazillionaire and I am happy to call you my friend!"

Carolyn laughed. "You have no idea how relieved I am. I just kept picturing all of the people who are depending on me as well as the money I'd spent. I was afraid I'd be back on my ass in Baltimore before Christmas."

"So what do you think you'll do now?"

Carolyn laughed, "I'm going to spend some money! I'm going to advertise and get us to capacity and hire another teacher. Them I'm going to hire some more help for the house and decorate the hell out of it for the holidays. You in?"

The two linked arms and headed for the dining room. "I am definitely in. Let's get that champagne!"

CHAPTER THIRTY-SEVEN

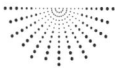

By the end of the day on Monday, Cindy and Ray were exhausted. The players were all in custody and the charges were being filed. They were ready to head home finally when Cindy stopped them outside the building. "You know what, this has been a really good day. Let's go share it with someone it will mean a lot to."

"Anyone I know?" Ray asked as they climbed into her car.

Cindy grinned. "Not yet, but you will." The drive out to the Lowe's residence didn't take long. There was a car parked in the driveway and what looked like every light in the house was on. They rang the bell and waited as a stereo was turned down and Pamela Lowe came to the door. Her face was such a contrast to the last time Cindy had seen it. She was almost unrecognizable. A wide grin spread across her face as she welcomed the agents in.

"Have you heard? Of course you've heard. You were probably behind it all. I got so excited watching the coverage on the news I had to leave work at noon. My sister's making cookies with my girls in the kitchen. I haven't told them why I'm so excited, but they're so glad to see me smiling at last that they don't really care."

She hugged Cindy briefly before releasing the agent and stepping back to close the door. "Can I get you something?"

Cindy shook her head. "No, we're fine, Pamela. Is there somewhere that we could talk quietly for a minute?"

"Sure, sure, come on into the dining room." She ushered them into the next room, clicked on the overhead light and then pulled out two chairs before taking one for herself. "Please, sit."

Cindy leaned forward and rested her hand on Pamela's. "I wanted you to know that everything you heard today, the arrests, the charges, it's all because of your husband, Arnie."

"What?" Pamela gasped and put her hand to her mouth. "How is that possible?"

"Your husband was a genius, Mrs. Lowe," Ray added. "It turned out he was keeping really meticulous records on the whole Warren enterprise."

"But how did you find them? Where?"

Cindy leaned back in her seat. "Arnie kept his word about not letting the information anywhere near you or your girls. He put all of it on a USB drive and hid it at Hammock's Beach State park. His friend, Greg, found it by accident."

"I can't believe it," Pamela breathed out. "Were you able to find out who killed him? Will they be on trial?"

Ray shook his head. "I'm sorry. We can't know for sure, but we think that the driver was killed down at the park this weekend."

"Wow, and Greg, you said was his name? Where is he? I'd like to thank him if I could."

Cindy smiled but chose to deflect the request. "He's in a hospital down in North Carolina now, but we'll be sure to let him know how grateful you are, how grateful we all are."

Pamela shook her head and then rose as the agents scraped their chairs back and stood to go. "I can't believe it, I just can't. I still miss him so much, you know? But now, I guess I just feel lighter. Thank you for coming out here to tell me. I know you didn't have to."

Pamela reached to hug Cindy once more, this time holding on for a moment longer. Then she smiled and saw them to the door.

Back in the car, Ray leaned over to give Cindy a long kiss. When he finally raised his head, he was beaming. "Have I told you yet that I'm falling in love with you, Agent O'Brien?"

"I don't believe you have, Agent Sanchez But it does seem like excellent timing, given that I seem to be falling in love with you right back."

"Yes!" He pumped his fist in celebration.

CHAPTER THIRTY-EIGHT

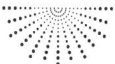

*T*he day before Thanksgiving dawned bright and crisp. Carolyn awoke way before her alarm, too excited to sleep any longer. They were having their celebration today so that people could travel the next. Rupert, Rusty and Helen were heading to her sister's in Philadelphia while Janine and April were going home to Baltimore to see Sean. In fact, Curt's fiancée, Brenda, was planning a meal for them at his house as well. So, in the morning, she and Angela would be busy making pies and a fruit salad to carry over for the meal.

As she lay there, stretching her arms and legs as far as they would go, Carolyn thought that there were an awful lot of amazing things to be thankful for this year. She knew that the money was a big part of it, especially now that it had been cleared for her to use, but it wasn't the only thing.

On Monday, she had been working at the desk in the classroom while her mother was reading stories to the children. There were more students than ever now that the center had really taken off, another blessing to be sure. She watched as her mother finished the wonderful book called *Creepy Carrots* and laughed as the children cheered right along with the victorious carrots. Afterwards, they were getting up and moving around when she saw a small girl named Ruby climb up into her mother's lap. She wasn't sure how Angela would react so she waited. Angela held the book open for the little girl to hold as she ran her hand lightly down the child's long hair. "You remind me so much of my beautiful little girl, Carolyn. I used to love to brush her long hair, it was just like yours."

The little girl grinned up at her before sliding down and heading off toward the bookshelves. Carolyn watched her mother stand and tuck the book back on the shelf before looking over at Carolyn. Angela gave her daughter a quick wink and then headed out of the classroom. Carolyn was practically speechless as she swallowed the lump in her throat and smiled a teary smile back at her mother. There was no way to know what the future held for Angela but it was clear that the present was bright.

Carolyn hopped out of bed, dashed through a quick shower and snuck out to the kitchen before PJ awoke. She wasn't surprised to find Helen already there, putting the beef roast into the oven. "Don't you ever sleep?"

The older woman laughed, closed the oven door and tucked a wispy gray strand of hair back behind her ear. "Good morning! There's coffee there if you're ready for it."

"You read my mind." Carolyn poured herself a cup and topped off the one that Helen had sitting on the counter. "Come, rest for a minute." Carolyn gestured to the stool beside her and Helen joined her. "You know, I woke up this morning thinking about all of the things I'm grateful for. You have to be at the top of that list." She raised her mug and clinked it gently to Helen's.

"No, no, it's me who's grateful." She set her mug down and gestured around her at the big open kitchen. "We loved Mr. Edward and I treasure all of the years that we had with him and his wife. But you," she paused, "you've brought the place to life again. That's what I'm grateful for."

Just then PJ came running into the room and jumped up onto

Carolyn's lap.

"Good morning, little man!"

"Hi, Helen. Hi, Mama!" Carolyn caught him up in a hug and blew tickling kisses on his neck until he giggled. She looked over the top of his head at Helen who was dabbing at her eye with the soft napkin.

Helen grinned. "You two go take a little time to yourselves before all of the guests arrive. My helpers will be here any minute."

Carolyn picked up her cup and a plate that held several slices of gingerbread. "All right, you little monster, let's get ready for this big day."

True to her word, the meal was ready and on the table at the stroke of one. It was amazing to see how the group had grown from that first morning when Carolyn had stood nervously in front of the massive door. Both doctor Gilberts were there along with Charlie and his friend Sadie. Angela was sitting beside April and Janine while Alex flanked PJ on his right. On the other side of them, next to Helen and Rupert and Rusty, were their most unexpected guests. Marybeth Rogers, her birth mother, had come along with her friend, Greg. He'd been released from the hospital just two weeks ago but seemed to be making excellent progress. He was chatting easily with Charlie and Janine and seemed perfectly happy to be where he was. From what she'd heard, there was a bright new future ahead of him now and he seemed to be moving into it with confidence.

They were all seated finally and Carolyn held her glass up high as they quieted. "I can't even tell you all how glad I am that you were able to join us here today. It's been rather an amazing year, don't you think?"

The group laughed and she heard 'hear hear' from Charlie. "Marybeth, you started all of this and there's no way to say thank you. And, Greg, you brought us all through it to safety and for that we'll be eternally grateful. Everyone at this table has made such a difference to my life and the lives of many more and I can't think of a better way to say thank you than with Thanksgiving. So, raise a glass to all of you, to the Center and to the future."

The glasses clinked around the table, PJ knocking his Sippy cup into any glass that he could reach. Laughter broke out then and the group settled down to eat. Later, once the last glass had been cleared and the guests ushered out, with PJ and April both down for naps, Carolyn finally had a minute alone with Alex. They had wandered back into the library and were sitting nestled in the chairs before a fire. "Look, it's snowing!" Carolyn pointed out at the garden.

"PJ will be thrilled. It's all he's been talking about lately."

"Don't I know it." It was such a relief now, the ease with which they could sit and talk. They'd even gone on a couple of dates. No one was taking any drastic steps or making predictions but Carolyn had to admit, it did feel right.

"So Carolyn, what *is* the story about the school and this house? I never did hear the full scoop."

Carolyn shifted in her seat, relieved now that the question had come back up, she finally felt ready to answer it. "The Edward Clark Children's Center was created in honor of PJ's Great-Great-Uncle Edward and is funded by a foundation that he established just before his death. My biological mother, Marybeth Rogers, and I are now the trustees of the foundation."

"Wow, that's a lot of responsibility."

Carolyn tilted her head, "I don't know about responsibility." She straightened. "It feels more like an honor to be honest."

"And the house?"

She laughed. "Yeah, there's something I have to tell you about the house..."

<<<< >>>>

ACKNOWLEDGMENTS

I would like to thank the Ann Arbor District Library and the staff of Fifth Avenue Press for this wonderful opportunity and the guidance that they have provided me throughout this process. They are an extraordinarily generous group of individuals and an asset to our local community.

I'd like to mention that the children's book *Creepy Carrots* is a Caldecott Medal winner written by Aaron Reynolds and illustrated by Peter Brown. It is one of my favorite books to read aloud to children.

I would also like to thank my family and friends who continue to offer their suggestions and encouragement. My husband David was this book's first reader and his comments as well as those from other friends and family provided much needed insight and support as I journeyed on with these characters.

Finally, I would like to extend a particular thank you to the staff and members of the Ann Arbor Curves. Their enthusiasm has been absolutely overwhelming. This community of women varies in age and background but shares a common core of warmth, strength and courage that teaches me each day what women are capable of doing.

ABOUT THE AUTHOR

Linda Cotton Jeffries grew up in Carlisle, Pennsylvania. She's a graduate of the University of North Carolina at Chapel Hill and was a special education teacher for more than 30 years. Linda lives in Ann Arbor, Michigan with her husband, and is surrounded by close family.

50153313R00149

Made in the USA
Middletown, DE
23 June 2019